CW00550970

Copyright © 2019 by Maya Daniels. All rights reserved.

No part of this book may be reproduced in any form or by any electronic or mechanical means, including information storage and retrieval systems, without written permission from the author, except for the use of brief quotations in a book review.

This book is a work of fiction. Any references, real places, real events, or real persons names and/or persona are used fictitiously. Everything in this story comes from the author's imagination and any similarities, whatsoever, with events both past and present, or persons living or dead, are purely coincidental.

Cover design by Jessica Allain, Enchanted Whispers

Interior design by Jessica Allain and Zoe Parker

Edited by Cassandra Fear

If you are unable to order paperback copy of this book from your local bookseller, you may contact the author at info@authormayadaniels.com or visit the website

www.authormayadaniels.com

to LOOK the DEVIL in the EYE

Maya Daniels

Chapter One

Helena

"She keeps hiding from me." Eric's frustrated growl carries through the hallway. "That woman will be the death of me. You'd think…" his words trail off along with the fading footsteps.

Blowing a breath through pursed lips, I sag against the wall, sliding down until my butt hits the floor. Okay, so I have been hiding. If he didn't keep pushing me to meet with Satanael, it wouldn't have been necessary, but he is as stubborn as I am. So, this is what we do now. Eric walks around the half-destroyed building where we've set up camp looking for me, and I run around, doing my best to avoid him.

I've jumped through a portal landing in Hell on a whim. I stood in front of Lucifer telling him to pull the stick out of his ass. I even jumped on the back of a dragon from Hell and fought against jinn. But the moment my father was mentioned, I turned into a blubbering idiot and ran.

And I'm not feeling bad about it either. Hell, no. It's so not happening.

"If you don't turn that judgmental mug away from me, I'm going to stab you, Narsi." Tracking my sidekick from the corner of my eye, I don't miss the deranged grin he sends my way.

"Satanael knows many secrets, mistress." Hissing, he crawls on all fours towards me. "It will be wise to hear his words."

"You know what's also wise?" Turning to glare at him stops him from moving closer. "To keep your mouth shut instead of lecturing me."

"Your father…"

"Hector is my father!" Snapping at him, my shoulders hunch with the anger hearing the damn word father associated with Satan brings me.

"The human has no idea what you are or what you need." Lifting on his feet for the first time, the Trowe grows a backbone for the first time when it comes to me.

"You need to hear Satanael's words more than he needs to speak them."

"And you know this how?" Narrowing my eyes, I watch the Trowe squirm. "What is it that you haven't told me?"

"You have a great responsibility, mistress." Dropping on his hands and knees again, he cocks his head like a bird. "I was bound not to speak your truth, but Satanael can tell you everything."

Closing my eyes, I thump my head on the wall in frustration. Everything in me rebels at the idea of facing Satanael. At the same time, guilt eats a hole in my stomach at knowing he is still trapped in that warehouse, waiting to see his daughter.

After the first day of not letting anyone near him until he saw me, he stopped being stupid and agreed to be freed. Eric got back a few hours later with burns all over his arms, his skin blistering and cracking as blood dripped in a trail behind him where he walked. He was so angry at me that day, even refusing help from his brother and the other two Fallen. All of them tried, but whatever was holding Satanael trapped was not easily removed. Maddison suggested she would give it a go, but Leviathan went a little nuts. Okay, he shifted into a dragon and started spitting fire all over the place, so that went out the window fast.

Now all of us are upset with each other, and avoidance is the theme of the week. All because I'm a coward.

Narsi perks up, stretching his neck and tilting his head left and right. Watching the Trowe is like seeing a car wreck. Horrible to look at, but no matter how hard you try, you simply can't pull your eyes away. You just stand there, horrified and fascinated at the same time.

"The hunters are back." His lips stretch into a terrible smile, too wide for his tiny face.

"Wha…" It takes me a second to comprehend what he said, but the moment understanding hits me, I scramble to my feet. "Let's go."

George and Cass have been gone for a few days. I refuse to think about them, too afraid that they'll meet their end if crossing paths with Mammon and his lackeys. Knowing that they are back is like a fog being lifted from my head. Forgetting that I'm still hiding from my mate, I rip the door open and bolt out of the room I've used for hiding. Colliding with a hard body, the air is pushed out of my lungs with a very loud *oomph*, ending up on my ass on the floor.

Narsi snickers.

"There you are." Eric reaches for me, pulling me to my feet.

"Oh." Giggling nervously, I slap his hands away. "Hey, monster boy. I didn't see you standing there."

"Which is the only reason that you are actually standing here with me." Clenching his fists, a muscle jumps in his jaw.

"I have no idea what you are talking about." Lifting my chin up, I stare him down.

"Really?" With a voice dry as a desert, Eric arches an eyebrow at me.

Narsi decides to burst into a fit of giggles at that exact moment, and we both turn to glare at him. Instead of cowering away, the crazy bugger starts jumping around, wiggling his body like he is trying to shake off flees. The giggles are high pitched, a sound that taunts me.

"I think he is going insane." Frowning, I watch my sidekick completely losing it in the hallway.

"She does not fear you, Shadow." Narsi keeps giggling, turning in circles like a dog chasing its tail. "No, she does not."

"He does have a point." Still watching the crazy show, I can't help but grin at Eric.

"You and this damn Haltija are a disaster waiting to happen." He growls the words but can't hide the corners of his lips twitching in a barely contained smile.

"He said George and Cass are back." Turning away from Narsi, I start down the hallway. "I need to see if everything is okay and if they brought someone back."

"You mean Hector?" Falling in step with me, I feel Eric's arm brushing mine.

It sends a pleasant shiver down my spine. The man is too hot for my sanity, and I'm not sure how much longer I can keep avoiding him. I miss his arms around me and his full lips on mine, but all that disappears the second I remember that he will start talking about Satanael.

"I do want to see Hector. To know that he is alive…" With a deep sigh, I rub my forehead, the building headache already pounding at my temples. "But I'll take anything at this point. As long as we get to save and protect some of them."

"Hel…" His warm, calloused fingers wrap around my arm, stopping me as he turns me to face him. "You can't keep taking responsibility for every life lost in this situation. All of us feel guilty that we should've seen it coming, but you…you let all of it tear at your heart like you are the one that caused all of this."

"It was me, Eric." My voice packs a lot of heat when I yank my arm away from him. "Or did you forget how all of this started? I will not shy away from my part in it. Everyone has every right to hate me and want me dead." The ground under our feet groans and shudders, forcing us both to stumble away from each other.

"Deep breaths, cupcake." Eric's voice is strained, even when he tries to lighten up the moment with that stupid nickname. "We will talk about all that later. I was coming to get you." When my eyes turn to slits, he smirks at me. "I knew where you were. I just figured you'd come to your senses and come out on your own."

"You and Shadow have a soul bond, mistress," Narsi hisses next to me, and I nudge him away with my boot.

"He can sense you when he is close, yes he can." Grinning that deranged smile, he looks from me to Eric.

"Tell me again why I keep him around?" The headache is getting worse.

"Because it's who you are, Helena." Threading his fingers through mine, Eric moves us along the hallway. "It's what I love and hate about you. You will stick your neck out for anyone, even those that don't deserve it. Although"—Glancing at the Trowe over his shoulder, he smiles, his handsome face lighting up with it—"the Haltija is useful, I must admit."

"You say that because he tries to bite Colt every time you get frustrated with your brother." Snorting, I shake my head, remembering Colt shouting for me to call off Narsi when he sneaked up in his room while he was sleeping and almost bit off half of his face. "The two of you act like two-year-old's."

"My brother will live." Grinning like a fool, he winks at me and my knees almost buckle. "It's a good thing we heal fast."

"Right." Shaking off the slack jaw and subtly wiping the little bit of drool from the corner of my mouth, I stare straight ahead.

I need to corner him somewhere, have my way with him, and then run before he opens his mouth to talk. That way, I won't listen to lectures, and I'll stop acting like I'm deprived. You might think that heat that burns in your veins when you start a relationship will eventually fade. That it'll become more bearable, so you can actually look at your other half without wanting to jump his bones. In our case, instead of fading away, it only burns hotter by the day. I can't even look at Eric without getting all hot and bothered, and his smoldering gaze tells me he feels the same. Even when we are ready to punch each other in the face.

Seeing the front doors of the building pulls me away from my hormonal insanity. The first thing I notice is Beelzebub's broad back blocking the doorway. Releasing Eric's hand, my feet speed up. Pushing the large Fallen is out of the question, so I squeeze through what little opening is left between him and the doorframe, screeching to a halt on top of the steps.

"What on earth is going on here?" My shout turns everyone's attention to me.

"I'll eat their face!" Narsi hisses next to me.

Chapter Two

"I will not stay here with demons!" a hunter I've seen around Sanctuary snaps, getting in George's face. I don't remember his name, but I never liked him; I know that much.

"Narsi, get your ass inside. You're not eating anyone." Grabbing the Trowe's hair, I hold him back, turning to Beelzebub. "Can you please lock him inside somewhere? He will only mess up this situation more than it already is."

"Look at her!" The jerk has spittle flying out of his mouth, his face turning red in anger. "You want us to become like her? Turn our back on Heaven? All your souls will burn in Hell for eternity."

"How melodramatic." I'm debating if letting Narsi loose will shut the idiot up. My headache is turning my vision blurry, and the loud yelling is not helping at all. "Unless you were hiding under a rock, you should know this has nothing to do with Heaven, or Hell for that matter."

About twenty or so hunters, all worse for wear with dirty uniforms and smudges of dirt and dried blood all over them, are huddled in one corner at the front of the building, eyeing me warily. Until recently, these were faces I've seen daily, and now those faces are eyeing me with suspicion that twists my stomach into knots. What's making it even more painful for me is that it reminds me of how I looked at Eric and Maddison when they were only trying to save my life. Giving Beelzebub an apologetic glance, I'm graced with an understanding smile on the Fallen's face.

"Talk to them." Taking Narsi by the scruff of his neck, Beelzebub urges me further into the front yard with a plate-sized hand on my back. "They are scared and confused. We don't know what they've seen or been through until your friends found them." Glancing at Eric, the corner of his mouth twists in displeasure. "And tell your mate to stop glaring at them. It's not going to help."

"You want them here?" I have no idea why I'm surprised by the large man at this point. He looks scary as hell with his size and red eyes, but so far, only understanding and support is what I've received from him.

"We can use all the help we can get, Helena." Turning away, he lifts the Trowe in the air and carries him kicking and wiggling inside.

Eric comes closer to my side, and I elbow him in the ribs. "Stop glaring at them."

"I don't like the way they are looking at you."

If there is one thing I know about, Eric, it's that no matter what is going on, if he sees someone even looking at me sideways he will stop to glare or punch them in the face for it, no matter if the world is ending or not. It's heartwarming and annoying at the same time.

"You don't have to like it." Moving closer to where Cass is doing a face-off with the hunters, her hands on her hips, my lips pucker and blow out a breath. "Just don't growl at them."

"I don't growl." The words are growly, and when I turn to pointedly look at his face, his lips flatten in a thin line. "I'll try."

Chuckling at his words, I stride next to my friends with my shoulders squared.

"I'm so happy you made it back safe." Reaching George, I give him a hug, his familiar scent and warmth calming my nerves.

His arms wrap around me, tightening like bands, and I feel his stiff body relax after a moment. I guess we both needed that—the comfort of a family—because that's exactly what we were to each other most of our lives. To my surprise, Eric grabs forearms with my friend, slapping his back. George nods once firmly, holding onto my mate's arm longer than necessary. That's when I notice how tired and worried he looks.

"You didn't come across any trouble, did you?" Half of my question gets muffled in Cass's hair when she almost tackles me to give me a hug.

"There is nothing left of the Order." My heart does a painful thump at the troubled look on George's face. "They are the only ones we could find. And we found them in the forest around Sanctuary when a few of them tried to attack us."

"Nothing is left because of the demons you want us to join," the jerk snarls from behind George.

"Listen to me, asshole." Pushing away from my friend, I get right up in the hunter's face. "No one will force you to stay here. All of us are fighting the demons that are trying to destroy Earth. If you think you have a better chance of doing it on your own, go right ahead. Get the hell out of here."

"No one in this place is going to hurt you. We are trying to keep you safe." With each word, I take a step closer to him, forcing him to step back. "When my life was on the line, I didn't see any of you stepping up to protect me. Unlike you, my soul—the one that will burn for eternity according to you—will not let me turn my back on you. I guess that makes me the biggest of evils you've ever seen."

"You are an abomination." The hunter finds his voice,

his shoulders curving inwards. "You opened the portal to Hell and brought this on our heads." Glancing over my shoulder, his face pales, and he stumbles back.

"Eric." Groaning, I rub my face. I don't have to turn to see him. Nothing can freak out a hunter more than a pissed off demon.

"I did not growl."

A humorless laugh bursts from me at his snapped words. My gaze flicks to Cass, and I can see she's barely hiding her own smile.

"Listen." Ignoring Eric, I look from face to face in the group of hunters. "Yes, I'm an abomination. No wishing or praying can change what I am. But I mean you no harm. This place"—Flinging a hand, I point at the building behind us—"is protected by wards. Nothing can hurt you here. It's a safe house…as safe as we can make it. Come inside. Eat, rest. And when you've seen for yourself, you can decide what you want to do. Nothing and no one will hold you here against your will. We are trying to fight against those that attacked the human realm. You can join us or stay and wait. We expect nothing from you. I just don't want you to die."

"And that is enough convincing. Now, you can do what you want." George grabs me by my shoulder and pulls me away from where I am facing the group. "I brought you here. It's up to you if you want to stay." Pushing me towards Eric, he grabs Cass by the arm and drags her with him. "I, on the other hand, am hungry and tired. I'm going inside."

Eric doesn't wait for more encouragement. As soon as I'm close enough to reach, he flings me in his arms, his long legs eating up the space to the open door within a second. Craning my neck, I see the hunters over his shoulder looking at each other. One by one, they gingerly move and follow us inside. I open my mouth to tell George, who is right on Eric's heels, that they are coming, but he shakes his head, shutting me up. A weight is lifted off my chest when all of them, including the jerk, enter the wards. He can hate me and be angry all he wants as long as they stay alive. I don't want Mammon or the jinn to take more lives than they already have.

My head rests on my mate's shoulder as I sigh. One disaster averted. Soon I'll have to sneak around again when Eric starts talking about Satanael. Another groan passes my lips at that thought. The hunters were freaking out about me being just an abomination. What will they do when they hear I'm Satan's daughter?

Chapter Three

Eric

"You look ready to bite that metal pipe, brother." Colt's words bellow around me, preceding him before he enters my space.

Ignoring him, I lift the two large slabs of a broken wall attached to each other by a metal bar. At least one thing is useful in the destroyed part of the building. A good workout can loosen up the tension brewing in my veins.

Drops of sweat trickle down the sides of my face, some of it dripping down my nose as I bare my teeth at my brother. Now is really not the time for him to instigate an argument with me. Time is ticking, I can feel it in my bones, yet I don't have it in me to push Helena to do something that she's not ready for.

I am a fool.

"Nah, you're just smitten." Snorting, Colt comes closer, plopping down on a pile of rubble and stretching out his legs.

Dropping the metal bar angrily, I barely miss my foot. With a string of curses, I swipe my forearm over my drenched face, glaring at him. For some reason, that amuses him more.

"I will not force her to meet Satanael." Snatching the bottle of water waiting for me on the side, I chug it down in one gulp. "She has been forced to do many things out of her control all her life. I will not add to it." Throwing the now-empty bottle at Colt's head, he swats it away, robbing me of the enjoyment I would've had if it hit him in the forehead. "I'll find another way to get him out of there."

"Do you talk to her the same way you are talking to me when you want me to do something?" Cocking his head to the side, he squints at me. "Because if the answer is yes, we are all fucked. She'll never do shit."

"You know nothing!" Snarling, I grab the crumpled t-shirt and wipe the sweat from my chest. The damn slabs were massive. Unfortunately, I don't feel less frustrated than I have been in the last few days.

It's Colt's fault.

He never knows when to leave someone alone,

sticking his nose in everything, which is one of the more significant reasons we were estranged until Helena turned my life upside down. A smile tries to push itself out on my face, and the look Colt gives me tells me he thinks I've finally lost my marbles.

"You can hold onto your grudge till kingdom come, Eric. We don't have time to let her run around the building like a youngling, thinking we don't know where she's hidden. Even without being able to feel her presence, the damn Haltija can't keep his mouth shut to save his life. The air is charged with something that I don't like." Nostrils flaring, all humor leaves his face. "Something is coming. And if both of you don't pull your heads out of your asses, we are all going to die."

My chest feels tight, as if I can't get enough air to enter my lungs at his words. I feel it, as well. Having it confirmed brings dread to the marrow of my bones, making my gut clench with anticipation and fear. If anyone told me I'd be afraid of a fight before I met my mate, I would've laughed in their face. Things have changed.

I've changed.

"I've been sitting around, hoping you'll come to your senses, but I'm out of patience." My brother continues to talk even when he knows his opinions are unwanted. "If you aren't going to do it, I will." Lifting his chin defiantly, he glares down his nose at me.

"She just needs time…"

"It doesn't matter what she needs. We need Satanael out of that shit hole. Now. Not tomorrow, not a few days from now." Lifting off of the ground, he dusts his pants with jerky movements, anger screaming with each twitch of his muscles. "If she is not ready to leave tonight, I'm going to have a talk with her."

Grinding my teeth to stumps, I watch his back until he disappears into the building. Filling my lungs with more air than they can contain, I lift my face to the skies, closing my eyes. He is right. It doesn't make things easier, but regardless of his shortcomings, I can't fault him for speaking up. Releasing the air harshly like a pricked balloon, with one last glance at the destruction around me, I head for the shower. Helena may never forgive me for pushing her, but we have no other choice. We have to follow the path fate forged for us long before we met. I just hope we come out of all this stronger.

The alternative is unacceptable.

Water still trickles down my neck, drenching the collar of my t-shirt from my wet hair when I find Helena leaning on the wall outside the front door, her arms wrapped around her bent knees. Stopping for a moment, I watch her solemn face as her eyes dart here and there, seeing everything and nothing at the same time. She is lost in thought, and the Haltija is nowhere near.

That is a blessing.

"You can sit if you like." She doesn't turn to look at me, and my gut clenches at the hollow sound of her voice.

"We need to talk." Our knees bump when I lower myself next to her, the heat of her body seeping into my skin.

"We do? How unexpected, monster boy." Sarcasm rings loud and clear in my words, and I can't hold back my smirk.

"You know what needs to happen, Hel." Pulling one of her hands to my thigh, I entwine our fingers together, giving her a reassuring squeeze. She stiffens for a moment before relaxing with a deep sigh. My heart breaks. "Why is it such a big deal to go meet him? If it were anyone else, I would've thought they were afraid. You, though. You stood up to my father like no one I have ever seen. Well, no one that still lives, I should say." I get my wish when she chuckles softly, shaking her head. "You faced off a jinn, Hel. How can this be any worse?"

"Knowing something is one thing, Eric." Leaning her head back, she closes her eyes, her long, thick lashes fanning her cheekbones, fluttering like the wings of a butterfly. " Having it undisputedly confirmed with your own eyes is a totally different story. I made peace that I had no parents. That they saw me so unworthy of their love or time that they left me like a discarded wrapper at the steps of the Sanctuary. I pushed it away, happy and grateful that Hector was kind enough to take me in. I spent my whole life proving to him that he made the right choice by accepting me." Her head turns, her green gaze finding mine, sending a shiver up and down my spine.

"Then he sought out the prince of Hell and ordered a hit on my life." A humorless chuckle makes her shake her head. "It's like the plot to a bad movie. And all that shit led me to find out that the actual Satan was my maker. If I were my mother, I would've gotten rid of me too, even if I wasn't an archangel."

"He is not what the humans make him out to be, Hel." Tugging on her hand, I wait until her eyes, sad and full of desperation, land on my face again. "I thought we were past this…that you had an understanding that things are not always black and white. We all have our roles to play in the great scheme of things. Such is the web of life and its creation." Frowning, I watch her free hand slide down her side, her fingers wrapping around the hilt of the dagger strapped to her thigh. "We don't have to make hasty decisions." Back peddling fast, my heart hammers against my ribs. She's not going to stab me, is she? Helena is fiery in her temper, and if it were any other weapon, I would've been a game. But that dagger will end me where I sit. Cold sweat trickles down my back. "We can give it more time if you need it."

"We will see him tonight." Her gaze is on my face, but her eyes are distant, unseeing. Uneasiness coils my body like a spring.

"What's wrong?" The words are just a breath leaving my unmoving lips.

"How fast can you get Colt and Beelzebub here?" She

finally returns her focus on me, and violence surges in my veins, answering the call for blood I see there.

"Fast enough." Unlacing our fingers, I'm already ready to get moving.

"Three of them are just outside the wards to our right. Get your brother here," Slowly lifting up as if nothing is wrong, she smiles at me. If I didn't know she was my mate, I would've shit my pants from that grin. "I think I can hold them back until you get here."

"Satanael won't know what hit him." Cursing under my breath, I bolt inside.

Chapter Four

Helena

Ignoring Eric's comment, I stride down the steps of the building. It's strange that he didn't notice the demons gathering so close I can almost see the crazed gleam in their beady eyes. I sometimes wonder if Eric is so focused on me when I'm around that everything else fades away. I worry it'll eventually cost him his life. Guilt and dread try to pool in my stomach, but I push them away. He is a big boy; he knows what he is doing.

I hope.

The air around me stirs, and the messed-up powers that swirl in my chest stretch my skin as if sunburned.

From the side of my eye, I see the demons shift uneasily, giving each other glances but not yet moving to prepare for an attack or bolt out of here. A few of them have been brave enough to come this close since we found this place. These idiots are either very strong or very stupid. I'm betting on stupid. The wards are stopping them from coming close to the building, but in a few steps, I'll be fair game.

I'm looking forward to it.

Flicking my hands to the sides, rolling my shoulders, I try to loosen up my stiff muscles. The anticipation of a fight doesn't help, churning inside me like lava. I have to push it down or I'll bring the building down on top of everyone's head when my power gushes out of me, rocking the ground under my feet. That will not help at all right now. In one fluid move, I exit the wards, turning in a slow circle as I look for more of the idiots in hiding. I see none apart from the three staring at me like I've lost my mind.

I guess they didn't think I was dumb enough to walk out of safety. The joke is on them. They should've done their homework better on all things that make Helena unstable. A grin stretches my lips, hurting my cheeks when I face them fully.

"Looking for me?" Their eyes zero in on the dagger I'm twirling in my hand.

"Mammon wants a word with you, girl." One of them, the leader I'm guessing, squares his shoulders.

These suckers are high level demons. Their bodies are large, the muscles bunching with each movement no matter how small. Their black eyes burn with malice on their flat faces, while rows of sharp teeth stand out stark on their shadowy faces since they can't hide their snarls. The leader has two stubs at his temples, telling me either someone chopped off his horns, or they are just starting to grow. It looks stupid on his face, regardless.

"He should've called to make an appointment. I'm a busy girl." Smirking at them, I keep twirling the dagger, the symbols on it coming to life and sending colors dancing around us.

One of them moves. Striking as fast as a snake, his giant claw-tipped hand reaches for me. Thanks to these crazy powers, he is too slow for me. My palm lifts in the air, blasting him in the chest. His body caves in, and he sails through the air, landing a few yards away on his back.

He doesn't get up.

"He wants to talk." The stub guy snarls at me. "You better hear what he has to say before you make the wrong choice, you ignorant girl. If you pick the wrong side, you and all your friends will die. Lucifer's son included." Gloating, a terrifying smile blooms on his face.

I match it.

"For that to happen, your daddy must kill me first, you dumbass."

"He is not…"

25

The demon doesn't finish his sentence. Pushing off the ground, I jump and spin, sending a round kick to his head, which snaps to the side, his body following it as he twirls in the air, dropping like a sack of rocks. The second demon throws himself at me, his claws out and ready to shred my skin. Not losing the momentum, I spin again, kicking my foot out and planting it in his gut. His body curves around my leg, and his sharp nails rip into my side. Being shorter than your opponent sometimes doesn't help.

Grinding my teeth so I don't cry out, I slash with the dagger, severing one hand at his elbow. A piercing shriek makes me stumble when he jerks away from me, his ugly face contoured in pain. Stars dance in front of my eyes when I get a blow to my head, dropping me on my knees. The stump guy recovered faster than I thought, I guess. Lifting my head, I see his rage-filled face too close for comfort a second before he is yanked away from my sight. Staggering to my feet, I see that Eric is back, his twin and Beelzebub on his heels.

"Keep one alive. Mammon sent them." Leaving them to deal with the assholes, I poke at my side. The blood is still fresh, soaking into my shirt, but the gashes the demon opened with his claws are closing up as I watch. Luckily, I didn't lose too much blood.

Eric grunts something, pummeling the stump guy to a pulp. I guess that one is not the one we are keeping alive. Beelzebub is like a tornado, flipping the armless demon in a circle with each punch to his face. It's funny to watch, but the anger inside me makes it impossible to laugh at the moment. These assholes came here intending to hurt the rest of the people we are trying to protect. If anyone else accidentally walked out of the wards without noticing them, they would've been dead.

"You are hurt." Colt's voice jolts me out of the anger I'm stewing in.

"I'm fine." Batting his hands away, I point at the crumpled demon further down the road. "I hope I didn't kill him. We can get Maddison to question that one since"—Looking at Eric and Beelzebub still playing with their punching bags, I grimace—"these two are done for."

"You didn't need us." Colt has no intention of moving away from me. "You could've dealt with the three of them on your own."

"And your point?" Lifting an eyebrow, I stare him down. "Did I interrupt your tea party or something?"

"You didn't want to fight them. You just kept them here until we came." His knowing gaze grinds on my nerves. "What's the matter, she devil? Lost your bloodlust?"

"Fuck you, Colt!" Spitting the words at him, I turn to leave.

"I would, with pleasure, Hel. But my brother would rip my dick off." Laughing, he follows behind me. "I'd rather keep my anatomy in check."

"You are disgusting." Shaking my head, I try to ignore

him, but it doesn't work. "There is seriously something wrong with you. And I told you to grab the demon."

"Eric will do it." When I turn my incredulous face his way, he laughs harder. "My brother needed to get his anger out first because they dared to harm his mate. He heard you, and like a good puppy, he will do as you ask."

"What's that supposed to mean?" My feet slow down until I stop to face him, my stomach dropping to my feet.

"Exactly what I said." Colt does not back down. "He would rather see all the realms, including this one, burn to ash before he does something to displease you. He's been walking on eggshells around you, giving you time—time we don't have need I remind you—so you can decide our fate."

Taking a step back, my jaw goes slack like he punched me. No words are coming out, although I want to scream at him and tell him where to shove it. He keeps talking, each word a blow to my heart.

"Poor Helena, she doesn't want to face her father. She needs time. Well, reality check, sweetheart. We have no time, and if we don't get Satanael out of that shithole to get to the bottom of this...none of us will live long enough to sulk about you having demon blood in you." His hands ball into fists. "Snap out of it, or you'll kill us all. Go fucking get that old fart moving before none of us stand a chance."

Shock makes me numb, and I watch him stomp away and disappear inside the building. Everything he said was like knife after knife shredding my soul. Is that what I've been doing? Selfishly sulking around while everyone held their breath, waiting to see what their fate is? Their future I decide for them with my actions. It shouldn't be news to me by now, but it's easy to get lost in my own head, dwelling on things I find essential. Things that don't matter when lives are at stake. A face becomes visible at the open door, and the hunter that was arguing with me stands still, watching me with an unreadable look on his face. How much of it did he see? Colt's words play on repeat in my head as I stand frozen, staring at the accusing eyes of a man that thinks I'm evil and not to be trusted.

"...none of us will live long enough..."

Chapter Five

"You look like you're about to puke or kill someone. I can't decide which one yet." Cass saddles up next to me.

I stay outside even after Eric comes back, dragging one demon by the leg like roadkill inside the building. Beelzebub is behind him, chest heaving and an exuberant smile on his face, but one look at me, and it disappears, making the guilt eat a hole in my chest. My mate says nothing. Just his deep green gaze searches my face, slowing him down for a moment before he looks away and disappears with his prisoner.

"What am I doing, Cass?" Eyeing her sideways, I

don't have the courage to look my friend in the face. "I never asked for this."

"None of us asked for it, Hel." Bumping her shoulder on mine, she blows a deep sigh through pursed lips. "Remember that time when Amanda got Jered drunk, and he ended up running through Sanctuary naked?"

An unwanted laugh bubbles out of me before I slap a hand over my mouth to stop it. My heart shrivels in my chest at the mention of Amanda and Jered. It's me and what I am that decided their fate, as well. The blood drains from my face.

"Hey!" Cass grabs my upper arms, shaking me. "I didn't mention that to make you feel guilty. None of this is on you, Hel. None of it, you hear me?" she snaps, her brown eyes sparkle with anger and determination. "It's those evil creatures that brought this on our heads. They took people we love from us. Not you. Never you."

"I started it all…"

"From what I heard, this whole shitstorm started long before you were born. So, as much as you've always had the spotlight, my friend, you can't hog this one. Sorry to be the one to tell you this."

As much as I don't want to smile, her stern and apologetic face pulls the corners of my lips up. She always had a way to lighten any situation. I shouldn't be surprised she can do it now, too.

"I keep thinking that they might be out there somewhere." Voicing it for the first time, I beg her without words to agree with me. "That we will find them eventually." She is shaking her head before I finish the sentence.

"No, we won't." There is finality in her voice that I've never heard before. "Jered is dead…I'm guessing Amanda is, too. Even if they kept her alive for a while, that woman could drive a saint insane. No way they let her live."

She allows me to search her gaze for a long time. Watching me unblinking, my eyes flick between hers, looking for something to tell me that there is doubt in her about what she is saying.

I find none.

"How can you be sure…" my voice trails off, while unshed tears fill her eyes.

"I killed Jared." Her voice is hollow, emotionless.

"Cass…" There is not enough air to fill my lungs as I try to come up with something to say. To call her a liar.

"The jinn didn't send us a copy of him, Hel." A fat tear trickles down her face, but she doesn't seem to notice. "It was him. The jinn only brought to the surface what has been pushed deep within his heart. He was always in the background, letting the rest of us lead, but deep down inside, he loathed us for it. He blamed his cowardice on everyone. Stewing in it while pretending it's what he wanted."

I open my mouth to tell her she is wrong, but a shake of her head makes the words die on my tongue. I watch my friend's heart torn to pieces through her devastated gaze. She doesn't cower from it, either. Cass allows me to see her pain with her chin up. Pride makes my chest tight.

"He said all that after you went through that portal. After George and I barely escaped with our lives. I shared myself with him. Got in people's faces to leave him alone and look what that got me. So, it was me that ended his life. When it came between my life or his, I chose me. I will not regret that." More tears slide down her cheeks. Mine follow as I swallow the lump in my throat. "What I'm trying to tell you is that this whole thing has nothing to do with right or wrong. Heaven, Hell, the fucking universe, you name it. These are three powerful factions fighting for supremacy, and we are the collateral damage. It's the survival of the fittest, Hel. And you know what?" Grabbing my upper arms again, her nails dig into my skin, the desperation in her eyes sending a bolt through my chest. "I say fuck them. Fuck all of them. Let's get this bitch lit like we always do, Hel. Let's show them who they are messing with."

Something inside me pushes forward, answering her call. My blood boils at the pain and desperation on my friend's face. Her breathing speeds up, matching mine as we stare at each other. We are a unit, and although two are missing, the three of us are strong enough to hold our own, even without my crazy powers manifesting and adding to the already-powerful punch. If she can stand tall in the face of all this, who am I to tell her no? Colt's words float through my mind again.

"...none of us will live long enough..."

"I need to make a choice to see Satanael, but I will not make any other choices for everyone else. Not even for their own good or to protect them." Taking a deep breath, I wipe the tears from my face with a forearm. "They can choose to join or go on their own. I'm done playing a scapegoat for everyone. If they want to risk their lives, they will have only themselves to blame."

"They've already made their choice." Cass loosens the tight grip she has on my arms.

"Not the hunters. They haven't." The unreadable face of the hunter pops in my mind's eye, watching me from the doorway. The air around us gets charged with power, the shadows dancing around us like they are coming alive. I don't need to turn around to know who has joined us.

"Yes, they have." A humorless chuckle comes out of Cass, sounding too harsh to my ears. "What are they going to do, huh? Hide in the trees for the rest of their lives? Eating roots? They made their choice when they followed us here. That idiot just wanted to be an asshole for no reason. I think you should go talk to that hot hunk of yours and let's get this shit moving."

"I think you just inflated his already huge ego." Cass looks confused for a second before she glances over my shoulder.

"Don't be upset with me for saying this"—A smile stretches her lips, all the pain and tears forgotten. I guess we both know how to hide our emotions—"but he is freaking hot. And you know the best part?" Bumping her shoulder on mine, her grin widens. "There are two of them."

A burst of laughter makes me double over. Looking over my shoulder, Eric glares at my friend like she just cursed him. Unable to stop myself, I laugh harder, my arms wrapping around my middle to stop the pain in my belly. Cass giggles too, her cheeks darkening to red, but she doesn't look away. Staring my mate down, she walks away, giving him a wink.

Eric growls.

"Colt is trouble. You should tell your friend." Grumbling under his breath, he watches her leave.

"So were you, and look at you now." Grinning at him, I reach a hand towards him, inviting him to join me.

Taking my offered hand, he pulls me to my feet instead. His arms wrap around me, tightening as I press my head in the hollow where his neck meets his shoulder. Breathing him in, my body sags against him. This is where I want to be always. Right in his arms. I want to forget about jinn and demons, archangels, and archdemons. I wish all of it to disappear and let me feel at peace. Because that is how Eric feels. Like peace and love.

Like home.

I open my mouth to tell him just that. To convince him to turn our backs and go on our own, to hide in whatever real he chooses. He will do it, too. Colt was not far off the mark when he called me out on my bullshit. I know that as well as I know my name. Eric will turn his back on everything, and he will take me away. What I hear myself say is not what I wanted to tell him.

"Let's go meet Satanael."

Chapter Six

Eric

I'm not sure what changed. Something is different in the way Helena's energy swirls around her. It's more stable, although it does burn like a bitch when it bursts out of her at random. She is still figuring out how to control it, and my chest swells with pride every time she grins at me after such an episode.

"Are we leaving?" Looking down the hallway, she seems like she's expecting others to join us.

"Yes, Hel." Taking her hand, I lead her outside. "It's just you and me."

"I thought your brother or Beelzebub would join us."

"Fewer people attract less attention." My skin prickles when we exit the wards. "No one has gone back to that warehouse after you defeated the jinn, but you never know. I would rather be cautious when it comes to you."

"I don't need you to baby me, Eric." Scoffing at me, she looks around, he muscles tensing as if she expects something to jump at us at any moment.

I feel the same.

My whole body is stiff, bracing for an attack. Until the three demons, things have been very quiet. Too quiet for my liking. Mammon sending those idiots to our door tells me he is ready to cause problems again. He can't stay silent for long, it's not in his nature.

"I'm not babying you." Tugging her along, I stop in front of one of the SUV's that we still have available for transport, debating the pros and cons of using it. "If that were the case, every single fighter in that house would've been around you."

"Good point." Releasing my hand, she drops on her knees, peering under it. "It looks clear."

A frown forms a line between her brows when she looks up at me. Her hair floats around her beautiful face, falling over her shoulders. The green gaze is sharp and no nonsense when my eyes drop to her swaying breasts. My pants feel tight seeing her like this, and the smirk on her lips tells me she didn't miss that.

"Keep your head out of the gutter, monster boy." Jumping up, she dusts off her hands on her thighs. "First, we meet daddy dearest. Then we can fuck."

Something has changed. I just don't know what, and it's pissing me off.

"Or, I can bend you over here for that foul mouth of yours." Snatching her to me, I grab her ass in my hands.

"Don't even try it." Pressing harder on my cock, she sways her hips seductively, eliciting a growl deep in my chest. "You love my foul mouth." Her full lips trail kisses up my neck until her teeth clamp on the shell of my ear. "Unfortunately, we must deal with this first, because when you take your clothes off, you won't be putting them back on for a while." The tip of her wet tongue flicks a few times before she pulls away. "Let's get this over with."

I'm so hard I can barely think straight. Her scent fills my nostrils, my shoulder blades tingling where my wings want to burst out so I can cocoon her in them and fuck her to oblivion. The vixen knows precisely what she is doing, and she will pay for it later. Right now, she is right. We need to get moving before more company shows up. With one last squeeze of her ass, I pull away. Yanking the door of the SUV open, I lift her in my arms before placing her on the seat.

Eyes dancing with amusement, she smiles, wetting her lower lip. This woman will be the death of me. Unable to ignore my primal instincts, I lean in, pushing her back deeper into the seat. As soon as my lips touch hers, she opens, her tongue tangling with mine. I kiss her hungrily, leaving no doubt in her mind what is to come when we get back. Her small hands claw at my shoulders, my heart thundering in my chest in sync with hers. For just a moment, I lose myself in everything that is Helena.

Her taste, her scent, the prickling power saturating the air around us is like fire ants crawling over my skin. My possessiveness is so strong it almost knocks me off my feet and steals my breath away. Pulling back for air, I press my forehead to hers, closing my eyes. Her chest is lifting and falling with fast breaths, short puffs of air bathing my face.

"If you only knew what you do to me." Taking her face in my hands, I bore into her half-lidded gaze. "I can live without the air to breathe, but I can't live without you."

"Ditto, monster boy." Taking a deep breath, she tries to compose herself. "It's a good thing you don't have to, huh? How very unfortunate for you." Sarcasm is dripping like honey from my lips.

A surprised laugh bursts through my lips. Shaking my head, I give her one more languid kiss before moving away and closing the door. I can feel her tracking my every move through the windshield as I round the front of the SUV and jump in beside her. Turning the engine on, I breathe through my nose, shifting uncomfortably in the seat. Driving with a rock hard erection is not fun at all.

Helena's giggle tells me she's very much aware of that fact.

All humor leaves me when we head through the streets of Atlanta. The once-beautiful city is in shambles. Swerving around large potholes, pieces of broken buildings, and tipped-sideways vehicles just further drives home the point of how screwed up this whole situation is. Helena's face is pressed to the window, her head moving left and right while she takes in her destroyed home. Sharp pain at the center of my chest almost doubles me over, and the car jerks to the left sharply before I get it under control. A damp, cold hand with icy fingers grabs my forearm.

My anchor.

Turning to look at Helena, I see her watching me with unshed tears shimmering in her eyes. The day is not entirely gone, the reds and oranges of the sunset making her look otherworldly, like a siren luring me with her gaze. Another sharp pain tightens my fingers on the steering wheel. My kind did this to her. To humankind. They destroyed everything she's ever known and want to kill her, too. I'll be damned ten ways from Hell if I let them anywhere near her. Heaven and Hell will burn together if a hair goes missing from her head.

"That's sweet, Eric, and I love you as much, but unfortunately, we will both get hurt many times before all this is over." Her cold fingers stroke my forearm. "The important thing is that we come out of it alive."

I wasn't aware I had spoken out loud.

"You will live through it, Hel." My words sound like an oath more than an assurance. "You will live if it's the last thing I do."

As always, fate is a bitch and loves a challenge when she hears one.

Chapter Seven

Helena

"Stop the car!" Grabbing Eric's arm, I squeeze the shit out of it.

Slamming his foot on the break, he almost sends me rolling between the seat and the dashboard in a heap. Slapping a hand on the dashboard, I stop myself from an embarrassment a second before he yanks me back, following it by shoving my head between my knees, folding me in half. Twisted like a pretzel, I'm not sure if I should laugh or stab his ass. Releasing a small surge of energy, I zap him, his yelp, and the hand disappearing

45

from the back of my neck, the only indication that it worked.

"Oh my God, I'm going to kill you." Shoving the hair out of my face, I glare at him. "You could have broken my neck like that dumbass."

He completely ignores me, his eyes moving rapidly while he searches the area for threats. "Why are we stopped?" His body seems like its growing in size, a muscle ticking on one side of his jaw.

Knowing I won't get through to him until he knows there is no threat out there, I turn to the window and press my nose on it. The movement I saw earlier is gone, the side street seemingly empty. I'm sure I didn't imagine it, but the longer nothing stirs, the more I shift in my seat. I'll never hear the end of it if it turns out I'm wrong. Much to my relief, Eric stays quiet, letting me wait it out. When nothing happens and I hear the crack of leather— which definitely tells me he is getting impatient—I'm ready to admit I was wrong.

Then I see it again.

"There!" Stabbing at the window, I squeak when my finger bends awkwardly. "Did you see it?"

Leaning to my side of the car, Eric's face comes next to mine. He doesn't speak, but his narrowed gaze misses nothing. His eyes glow for a second when he finally spots what got my attention.

"Humans." My throat tightens with emotion. "They are alive, and they are going to fight back."

Eric says nothing, but he doesn't have to. The shadows on the street, and in the car, start moving, coming to life. His skin stretches tighter on his face, his cheekbones sharpening.

"Oh shit!" He is about to change, and the space is not large enough for both of us in here. "Shit…fuck…"

Not knowing what else to do apart from cursing up a storm, I grab his face and slap my mouth on his. His whole body turns, his tongue diving deep between my lips. Under my fingers, I feel the skin softening slightly until he is back under control. Feeling confident he is going to be okay, I pull back…

And I slap him.

The sound echoes in the enclosed space, and Eric's eyes widen comically. My palm is tingling from the force of the slap, which would've been hilarious if my heart was not in my throat.

"You would've squashed me like a bug, you ass."

"The human…" His voice is still rough, the change not far enough away from the surface yet.

"Yes, he was military. But don't you see?" Excitement bubbles up again inside me. "They will fight back. They will be on our side."

"You mean to tell me they'll be able to see a big enough difference between demons and the Fallen so they don't accidentally shoot the good guys?"

And just like that, he kills my joy.

I hate it when he is right.

"If we maybe talk to them…" My words trail off because I already know that is not going to work.

"We need to stay away from them, Hel." His face softens. "I know you grew up among them, but you are not human." Reaching up, he pulls my hand away from my mouth. I wasn't even aware I was biting my nails. "You never were one of them."

"It doesn't matter." Pushing away from the disappointment and the fact that I'm not human, I lift my chin up. "They are fighting back. It'll divide Mammon's attention, at least."

"We will tell Maddison. She'll keep an eye on things." Settling back in his seat, he starts the car and we move again.

My head turns, and I keep staring behind us until we make a left turn, losing sight of the side street. Regardless if Eric is right, this must be a good thing. If nothing else, I'm just happy to see some humans alive. All this time, I pushed the thought of them away, unwilling to consider that they are dead. Or worse, captured and tortured somewhere.

We hit the side of a crater like pothole and it jostled us around in our seats. Eric curses up a storm, my ears burning red when he describes in detail what Mammon should do to his mother. A crazed laugh bubbles in my chest, bursting out of me before I can stop it.

Speaking of a mother…

"You think she's alive too?" The sound of my insanity cuts of when I face Eric with a somber face.

He does a double take, the curl on his lips dropping. Taking a deep breath, I watch his arms flex, his fingers clenching and unclenching on the steering wheel. My stomach churns, bile-like acid rising in the back of my throat. I regret the question immediately. He answers it anyway.

"I might be wrong, Hel." Keeping his eyes locked on the road, Eric won't look at me. "But, I think not." His jaw works for a while, no words coming out until finally, more to himself than to me, he adds, "Zadkiel was a force to be reckoned with. No jinn, nothing could hold her down for long."

"We thought the same of Satanael." I can't help pointing out.

"He is more valuable alive. I had no doubt he will resurface." Finally, glancing at me, he reaches for my hand, wrapping his warm fingers around mine. "Your mother, on the other hand, would've slaughtered them all the first chance she got. She would've put them all out of their misery, as was her way. She was the mercy of God, his personal weapon, after all."

"You make her sound more terrifying than the Devil." An uneasy chuckle sounds dead to my ears.

A smile stretches Eric's lips, making my heart do a fast, double thump against my ribs. "Oh, but she was… In many ways, she was someone everyone feared."

"And yet she's dead." Turning to stare out the window, my brain feels numb to it all. This is why I don't like thinking about the two that gave me life. It makes me wish they didn't.

"Some of her maybe." Eric takes a sharp right turn, avoiding a pile of rubble on the road. "But not all of her is gone."

He hits the breaks before I can question him further. Still, I open my mouth to say something when the stiffening of his shoulders makes my head whip around to look in the direction of his stare. With a groan, I bury my face in my hands, rubbing it roughly.

"I bet you wish you babied me now, don't you." My words are muffled through my fingers, and I don't need to see him to feel his glare stabbing the side of my head. Another crazed laugh bursts from my lips. "What do you want to bet Narsi will find us before all of this is over?"

"If that little fucker shows up, I'm going to rip his head off myself." The steering wheel groans painfully, and Eric curses under his breath.

Peeking through my fingers, I laugh out loud, dropping my hands in my lap. The perfect circle is bent and twisted, almost like an infinity symbol. Eric's hands are still clutching it as if he is strangling the poor thing. Still giggling, my gaze turns to look at the warehouse across the street, just a few buildings down the road. A dozen or more demons patrol it, some of them perched on the roof while others stomp on the ground. I didn't want to face my father, but now that I'm here, anger burns like a bonfire in my chest.

"I guess Mammon was expecting us." I gasp when a burst of my power gushes out of me, charging up the air in the car.

"It appears so." Eric, as always, reacts to it, his protectiveness making him as terrifying, as he is handsome.

"Let's get out of the car before your wings pop out." Fumbling with the handle, I push the door open, jumping out as fast as I can. "I don't want to fight demons with feathers stuck in my teeth."

With a horrifying chuckle sounding like rocks grinding together, Eric exits his side of the car. The sound of wings popping out and unfolding reaches my ears. A shiver runs up and down my spine, my core heating up, forcing me to press my thighs together.

The Prince of Hell just arrived, and he is pissed.

Chapter Eight

"Stand back."

Walking a few steps ahead of me, the jackass spreads his wings, hiding me from view. Pursing my lips, I hold my tongue for exactly two steps. Left, right.

"Last time you tried to pull this shit, it didn't work out well for you." Reminding him that this is a fight he will not win does not deter him one bit.

His black wings spread out more, making me wonder how the weight of the enormous appendages doesn't topple him over. Spread out, they are as long as two Eric's standing one on top of another. His body prowls down the street as graceful as a dancer, the width of his wings moving in perfect sync with it. It's mesmerizing to watch. Shaking my head, I glare at the back of his head. He knows how much I love his wings, and by ruffling them, he is trying to distract me.

"I'm going to stab you in the ass, Eric." My fingers are already wrapping around the hilt of my dagger. "You are such a jerk."

When I step closer to him, his wings snap back to fold over his shoulders, and he dances away for a few steps. He is smirking at me, but there is wariness in his gaze. He knows I'm not joking. Maybe I won't do it with this dagger, but I'll find one that he can heal from.

"And you are easy to rile up, cupcake." His deep laughter is like boulders tumbling down a hill, vibrating in my chest.

"Let's kick some ass." Rolling my shoulders, I let the anger surge up to the surface, an easy feat with those idiots right in front of me.

The ground under our feet shudders.

"I love the feel of your power." Eric's heated gaze finds mine, causing tingles to erupt all over my body.

"Yeah, I'll remind you of that next time you yelp like a little girl."

Snickering at his scowl, I gloat. It's funny that in his human form, my power burns him just like everyone else. He doesn't shy away from it, thankfully, but I'm sure it's unpleasant. Only when his wings and horns are out does he soak it up like a sponge. Something to think about when our lives are not in danger.

The dumbass demons finally spot us strolling down the middle of the road like we own the place. Cass's words about showing them who they're messing with sends another surge through me, shuddering the earth beneath our feet. Eric growls low in his throat, and when a couple of the demons lose their balance and drop on their ass, I grin.

Another surge of energy, potent and very different from the first, bubbles in my veins. I didn't notice it at first, but something in that building is calling to me. Not like a trap, no. It's soothing and welcoming, gentle ghostly fingers probing at my powers, testing. Checking if I am what it expects me to be.

What it wishes I am.

Shaking my head to clear it, I frown at the gray, dull warehouse. What the hell is going on? If there is another jinn in there trying to mess with my head, I'm going to go nuts and destroy everything here along with it. I've had enough of those assholes.

"Let's hope they didn't have time to move Satanael from here." Eric's words are like a lightbulb in my head.

"He is here."

Excitement and dread mix together, but I'm one-hundred percent sure I'm telling Eric the truth. Those probing fingers were him, his power, checking to see if I am his daughter or an imposter. With jinn running around pretending to be everyone and their brother, I can't say that I blame him. Thankfully Eric, getting smarter by the minute, doesn't question me. With just one sharp nod, he squares his shoulders, lengthening his stride. I have to jog to keep up with him.

Twirling the blade, I watch with a smile when it lights up, sending a rainbow of colors dancing around us like a disco ball. Some of the demons jerk back, their eyes widening before they bolt out of there so fast I can barely see which way they went. The ones that were perched on the roof like some stone gargoyles drop down with a thump, straightening and preparing for a fight.

Eyeing the double doors of the warehouse, I see there is no way to get inside without killing all of the demons first. How nice that Satan will meet his daughter for the first time covered in blood and guts like some wild animal. There will be no doubt in his mind, power testing or not who the Devil's daughter is. A peal of hysterical laughter makes Eric jerk his head my way, watching me like I've lost my mind.

Maybe I have.

"You take a right; I got the left." Reaching the first line of demons, I release my carefully held control over my powers.

Two opposing sides crash inside my chest. The concrete under my feet trembles, cracking down the middle with the vein in it spreading all the way to the building between the bunch of demons. I hear Eric's pissed-off roar like a clap of thunder rolling over me before he tackles a handful of demons, plowing through them like a truck. His wings are snapping, sending those closest to him flying in the air like dolls. Leaving him to do his thing, I throw myself at the first demon, my hand slashing in an arch as my body sails through the air. His head rolls off his shoulders before my feet touch the ground.

His body standing next to him snaps its face up, looking at me with horror-filled eyes.

"Playtime, motherfucker."

Eric's laughter makes me giggle as I slash at the other demon, splitting him open from navel to neck. Twisting around, I reverse round kick the other coming at my back. The rest snap out of their shock, swarming me like vultures. Their large bodies and swinging arms get in their way, allowing me to bend, twist, and turn to avoid most of the hits. Pain sears my skin as claws rake my arms and back. My dagger is slashing with each breath I take, the pained roars and grunts telling me I have found my target. It's hard not to. I'm surrounded by demons, their size blotting out the little light there is from a couple of street lamps on either side of the building.

"Don't kill her." One of the demons from the back grunts. "Capture her."

Another set of claws sink into my thigh before my foot connects with the demon's gut. I double him over, but not before he does a number on my leg. Biting my lip to the point where I can taste my own blood, I rip my leg away from him, bright spots dancing at the corners of my eyes. Like hell I'll let them capture me. I will rather slit my own throat right here.

Eric's rage-filled roar bursts a few windows of the warehouse. Glass shatters, the sound of the breaking and raining shards so out of place in this horrible place. It's like tinkling, cheerful music in the middle of a funeral. Slashing sharply to my right, I sever the demon's leg that was heading right for my injured thigh. Dizziness makes me sway on my feet a second before my skin crawls from the touch of the demon that grabs me by the arm from behind. The two opposing powers in my chest that were trying to fight each other for dominance snap to attention, twining together and blasting out of me like a dam has been broken.

Bright lights force my eyes closed, almost as if I'm staring at the sun. The dagger heats up in my hand, fusing the hilt to my palm. Numbing pain does not even allow me to scream, but it's all gone in a second, the bubble of silence around me bursting. Shrieks and screams fill my ears, and my eyes snap open just in time to see the demons bursting up in flames.

Fire.

Tall flames are rising towards the sky, decimating everything around me. The fires are not their usual red and orange, making my heart lodge in my throat. Deep red that is almost black flickers around me, bright blue and white webs spreading through it. No smoke comes out of it, yet the more I watch, the bigger the flames get.

Oh my God. Eric! I killed Eric! my mind screams in panic, my feet moving to send me stumbling towards the flames. If I hurt my mate, I will go out right beside him.

The strange fire darkens in one spot, something in the shape of a man moving through it. A scream with Eric's name gets stuck in my windpipe, the words dying on my tongue when the flames part.

Eric walks through the fire, determination etched on his handsome face. His wings flare around him, pushing the flames like they are made of molasses, the edges of his feathers sizzling from it. His eyes are a raging inferno when they settle on my face before flicking to my injured leg. He throws his head back, releasing another terrifying roar. The two sets of horns on his head seem to grow in size, his hair wild and tangled around them.

He has never looked more beautiful.

In two strides, he stops in front of me, staring me down, his fingers twitching as if he is unsure if he should touch me. I'm not sure myself that it's a good idea. My mouth works soundlessly for a moment before I hear myself speak.

"The fire did not burn you." My voice sounds strange, like angels singing in the background. *What the hell is going on?*

"I would've walked through it even if it did." Eric's

gaze is so intent it's like he is trying to see straight inside soul.

"The moment you lose your way, it will burn you." Mind spinning, I can't believe what's coming out of my mouth.

"The moment that happens, I'll deserve it." He is still standing one step away from me, not coming closer. His body is as coiled as a spring ready to snap.

This whole thing is surreal.

"You don't have time. They are coming." Watching Eric nod, I just gape like a fish, not understanding anything. Maybe I lost too much blood and I'm hallucinating. That's it! It's known to happen. "Look after her, Shadow, or you will know pain like no other."

"With my life." Eric bows his head, and dark spots dance in front of my eyes when the weird energy pumping through me disappears with a whoosh.

"Eric…" My gasp is barely a whisper. I'm already wrapped in Eric's arms, confusion making my heart jackknife in my chest.

"I got you, Hel." Tightening his arms, his wings curl up around us, plunging me in darkness. "I got you."

Chapter Nine

I'm drifting in and out of a dreamlike state, forcing myself to snap out of it and stay conscious. Now is not the right time to leave Eric to fight on his own if the demons return.

What's left of them at least.

"Let...I want...up..." mumbling incoherently, I'm trying to push away his arms that hold me down.

"Take it easy, Hel." Eric keeps murmuring encouraging words, his voice calming down the panic that is building inside me.

I can't see anything.

"I'm blind." A sob rips from my chest, and fat, hot tears trickle down my face.

Whatever that power was, it took my sight. Damn, it almost took my life.

"You are not blind." He chuckles uneasily. "I have my wings around you."

I keep wiggling in his arms until he finally releases the vice like grip he has on me. Weak, yellowish light penetrates the darkness when he shifts, and I latch onto that with everything I have. *I'm not blind!* That thought makes me more aware, snapping me back to the present and into my own body. The feeling slowly returns to my limbs, my skin tingling so much it is almost as if I had been frozen and am defrosting right now. As uncomfortable as it is, I'm happy to move without flopping like a fish.

"We need to get out of the open." Lifting my head, I see Eric watching me with concern. It's a little unnerving on his sharp, angled face and horned head.

"Can you stand?" His hands hover around me when I push off the ground so he can catch me before I introduce my face to the nasty pavement.

"I think so." Breathing through my nose, I stiffen my legs and pull myself to standing. The street sways for a moment, everything around me swirling in a loop before I blink it away. "What the hell was that Eric?" Pointing a shaking finger at his face—well, more like at his crotch, but who cares—I cut off his lies. "And don't say nothing because that sure as hell was not me talking. Like, what the fuck?"

"If you can walk, let's get inside the warehouse to see if Satanael is still there. We can talk about it when we are not standing in the middle of the street." He shifts around, ready to carry me if I refuse to move.

"What the hell is the matter with you? Are you crazy?" Fear claws at my throat of what I could've done to him. "I could've killed you, you asshole."

"I'm perfectly fine, as you can see." His lips flatten in a thin line, giving his face a more severe look.

"I could've burned your balls off." Glaring, my nostrils flare in anger.

"You need my balls," Eric says, dryly.

"Exactly!" snapping, I look away from him and finally see what I've done to the area.

The street looks like someone decided to dig a tunnel to the center of the earth. Slabs of concrete are lifted in quite a few places around large, gaping holes. The SUV further down the road where we left it is tipped on its side, surrounded by shards of broken glass. Even the sparse trees that were standing tall here and there now look like some morbid Halloween decoration, charred, with black trunks and gnarled branches, like twisted fingers reaching for the sky.

Oh my God…I did this.

"Let's get inside," Eric repeats, taking a step closer to me.

"Stay back." Stumbling a few steps, I stare at him wide-eyed. "There is something seriously wrong with me." He takes another step, and the ground quakes under our feet. "Stand back, Eric! I'm dangerous, and I don't want to hurt you."

"You won't." Jaw clenched, he closes the distance between us, grabbing me by the arms. " Breathe!"

The touch of his skin, his scent filling my lungs, calms down my gasping. I wasn't even aware that I sounded like a frightened little rabbit until my panic disappears. Not taking my eyes off him, I continue to take long, deep breathes.

"This is insane." I can feel my heart beating in my throat.

"It's just bad timing, Hel." Leaning closer, he presses his lips on my forehead. "Just breathe. Everything will be okay."

"What was that?" Closing my eyes, I sag in his grip, and he gathers me in his arms.

"I think your life being in danger, combined with you being so close to your father, brought out your mother's powers out, too."

"That did not look like a heavenly fire to me." A shiver races up and down my spine, making me tremble in Eric's arms.

"No, it was much more than that." Mumbling, his chin taps the crown of my head, his voice vibrating in his chest where my face is firmly pressed. "It was Heaven and Hell rising up to protect you. I never thought I'd see something like that."

"That was not me talking." I can't let that one go. It freaked me out so bad I want to start scratching at my skin to get it out of me. Whatever it is.

"No, it wasn't." When it becomes evident that Eric is not going to elaborate on it, I huff out a sigh.

I guess I'll just have to interrogate Satanael about it. My stomach does a somersault at the thought, and I want to puke. But, for better or for worse, I came all the way here and almost destroyed the neighborhood, so I might as well get it over and done with. Plus, we can use all the help we can get. The jinn have been quiet after our last fight, but that doesn't mean they'll tuck tail and run. No, they are brewing something.

"Here."

Eric steps away, and I frown at him, not understanding what he is on about at first. Until my eyes flick down to his raised arm. There, in his giant claw-tipped hand, he is clutching my dagger. My heart skips a beat, and my gaze jerks to his face. Seeing his jaw clenched with a muscle spasming does not make me feel happy. He always stays as far away from as he can get.

"You dropped it when you fell." His hand shifts forward, wanting me to take my weapon.

Keeping my focus on his face, I reach out and wrap my fingers over his. We both hang onto it now, Eric's eyes glowing slightly as he stares at the dagger. The symbols glow, giving us a light show, the swirling colors dancing across our faces.

Eric's fingers tighten on the hilt.

"I got it." Keeping my voice even, I continue to watch his face. That muscle is still jumping on his jaw.

"It's yours. You shouldn't drop it like that." His grave words do not match the longing look in his eyes.

"Let it go, Eric." Pushing my fingers harder through his, I feel that weird energy poke it's head inside my chest. "I'm going to burn your ass if you don't let go now." His eyes jump to my face at those words, and I give him a humorless smile. "And after I burn your ass, I'm going to stab you with this same dagger." Grinding my teeth, I yank on the blade. "Drop it now."

Eric's entire body flings away from me when he unwraps his fingers from my weapon. His eyes look wild when he stares at me, and my chest tightens at the panic on his face.

"It's fine, you gave it back." Shoving the thing in the holster wrapped around my thigh, I reach for him. "It's okay, Eric."

"So much power." Swallowing thickly, his shoulders stiffen. "It's impossible to resist it, Hel."

"But you still did." Blowing out a breath, I roll my neck. "You can be an asshole most of the time, but you have a good heart, Eric." When he lifts a sharp, protruding eyebrow at me, I grimace. "A kind heart when it comes to me?"

A surprised laugh bursts out of him, and he shakes his

head. "Only a fool wouldn't have a kind heart for you, Hel."

"Remember to tell that to Mammon when we find him. I'm sure he will change his ways." With a halfhearted giggle, I turn to look at the warehouse. A chasm opens in my chest. "Let's go in before I change my mind." Taking one step, then another, I feel Eric right behind me. "If worse comes to worst, I can always stab his ass instead of yours."

Eric laughs, and my lips twitch at the corners. That's as much as I manage before all humor leaves me. There is nothing funny about this situation. Nor is there any way of avoiding it. Steeling my nerves, I take a deep breath as we reach the two metal double doors of the building. Eric's hand presses on my shoulder in silent support.

I push the doors open.

Chapter Ten

The moment I force the doors open, something slams into my back, sending me toppling to the side. Curling my shoulders inward, I tuck and roll, hitting something hard before I can stop. A reverberating sound like the plucked string of a guitar sounds in the silence that follows, barely audible from the thundering of my heart.

A crash, then the sound of wood breaking echoes from the depths of the dark warehouse, a few yelps and roars accompanying it. My head snaps to the side to see a long ass piece of a plank, almost as long as my arm, sticking out of the spot where my head should've been. I lose sight of it when a black wing gets shoved in my face. Batting

Eric's appendage with both hands, I struggle to get out from behind him, shuffling on my knees and glaring at the side of his head.

He ignores me.

Crouched like a sprinter ready to bolt for a hundred-meter run at the Olympics, one hand pressed down and fingers touching the floor between his feet, he moves his head slowly from side to side. His black wings flutter stretched out behind him when his chin lifts slightly, nostrils flaring. His gaze flicks to my face.

"Stand back, Hel. We are not alone." Lifting himself up, he reaches for me.

"No shit we are not alone." Grumbling under my breath, I slap his paw-sized hand away. "I can stand on my own, thank you very much."

A movement I notice from the corner of my eyes gets my attention before any more words leave my mouth. My hand slaps my forehead, and a pained groan passes my lips when a small head toppled with messy blond curls pops out from behind a large crate that I didn't notice until now.

"I should've forced you to make that bet." Pushing the words through clenched teeth at Eric, I scowl at Narsi, who is grinning at me like he just won an award.

"I ate their face, mistress." The Trowe hisses happily, churning my stomach.

"This can't be my normal." Mumbling under my breath, I eye my sidekick warily. "It just can't."

Eric snorts, shaking his horned head. Tucking his wings close to his sides, he wiggles his fingers in my face for me to take them, so he can help me up. A crazy thought hits me, and a nervous, hysterical giggle from me makes him frown slightly as if doubting my sanity. Even Narsi stops grinning like an idiot, tilting his head to the side like some weird bird.

"My sidekick gets off on eating faces, my mate has horns on his head, and I'm about to meet my father, the Devil." Another giggle makes me look nervously around. "It sounds like the start of a bad horror movie."

"We can come back tomorrow." Eric's jaw clenches, and I can see that the stubborn ass is about to pull some macho shit on me. "It's a trap. With a few of the others, we will have a better chance of getting Satanael out of here in one piece." Bending slightly, he grabs my arm and pulls me like a doll.

It has nothing to do with this being a trap, and we both know it. I've never met anyone so thrilled to be in the middle of an ambush. You'd think his only purpose in life is to dance with death without and give the cloaked bugger a taste of his prize. No, this is him being an overprotective asshole.

As always.

Yanking my arm away, I turn to the Trowe, ignoring my mate. Eric grunts something that sounds a lot like a curse, but he knows better than to keep pushing. My fingers twitch around the hilt of my blade.

"How many were there?" Looking past Narsi, I finally get a good look at the inside of the warehouse.

The only light comes from the open double doors, casting strange shadows over everything. What shocks me most is that the vast open space looks more like some reception area. Getting off my knees, I stand up before sticking my head out to see better. Chairs are tipped sideways in few corners, smooth, windowless walls with paintings on them stretching on two sides with a couple of short, potted trees sprinkled around it. Large wooden crates are stacked around as if this place is planning an exhibit or they're leaving and waiting for the movers to come pick their shit up.

"Three, mistress." Narsi hobbles out from around the crate, latching onto my leg.

Something drops on the other end of the vast space, crashing to the floor. Eric's wings shoot out in front of me, sending me stumbling back. Having Narsi clinging like a koala doesn't help, and I almost end up on my ass.

"Move those wings out of my face Eric, or so help me God, I'm going to rip them off one feather at a time." The ground under our feet shudders.

Thanks to the Trowe's fast reaction when he pushed me out of the arrow's way, we are hidden in the shadows, a stack of the crates shrouding us from view and keeping us away from the yellow light coming through the open doors. Still, the longer we stand here talking, the more trouble will come our way.

"Narsi, can you go ahead and see what's waiting for us?" Cringing at the word "see," I glance at his eyeless sockets and give him a tight smile. "Or smell...or whatever it is you do." Finishing lamely, my lips twist in a grimace.

"There are hellhounds, mistress." My stomach drops to my feet at the terrifying smile on his face. Eric's head snaps over his shoulder, and he glares at my sidekick.

"What?" The question is barely a breath exiting my lungs as I stare at the Trowe, cold sweat trickling down my back. "What did you say?"

"Hellhounds." Hissing, Narsi's smile excitedly stretches wider, almost splitting his face.

"What the hell is the matter with you?" Spitting at him angrily, I grab a fistful of his hair to yank him off my leg. "We don't get excited about hellhounds, dumbass. They are bad...like very bad."

Wiggling so I can put him down to latch onto me again, no doubt, Narsi pouts.

"So Lucifer is involved in this shitstorm, after all." Ignoring my sidekick, I watch Eric turn around with a frown on his face. "He said hellhounds." Jerking my hand at him, the one holding Narsi a foot off the floor, I shake the Trowe in his face, just in case he doesn't remember who told us that.

"The hounds are connected to Hell itself, not to my father." Eric's frown deepens when Narsi almost kicks him in his attempts to get lose from my hold. "They are mindless creatures following orders. If someone is not meant to leave Hell or left the realm without permission, they are sent to retrieve them…at all costs."

I can tell his mind is on Satanael, but dread pools in my stomach. Eric has permission to be here because of his argument with his father. But he was hurt when we got back from Hell together and won't even think about what I did so I can keep all of us alive. His own brother, Narsi, Beelzebub, and Leviathan, all left their realm without Lucifer giving the green light. Not like we could get approval even if we wanted it. One: We were trying to escape with our heads still attached to our shoulders. Two: Lucifer was missing thanks to those murderous jinns.

With that thought, I yank my hand back, hugging my sidekick like a two-year-old getting their hands on a kitten for the first time. I'm practically strangling the Trowe, but he doesn't mind, wrapping his tiny arms around me and clinging like a monkey.

"No." There is so much venom in my voice that Eric takes a step back, his eyes like saucers on his face. "They will not take them anywhere. Who orders them if Lucifer is not there?"

Understanding dawns on his face, which comes after his initial reaction of confusion when I hug my sidekick, squeezing him so hard he can barely breathe. Groaning, he rubs a hand roughly over his face, glancing around uneasily.

"Any of the seven fallen can order it in my father's

absence. Fuck!" Exploding, his arm shoots out, breaking a fist-sized hole in the crate.

"We are trying to hide from hellhounds." My voice is as dry as sandpaper, and I look pointedly at his fist that is still stuck in the crate.

"If they were going to attack, they would've by now." It takes two tries for Eric to get his fist out of the hole. If shit weren't so messed up, I would've laughed. "I'm guessing they will stay in the shadows to follow us back to the others."

Narsi's bony fingers tighten on my back. He is snuggled in and practically purring on my chest. As creepy as he is—and I must admit horrible to look at—the Trowe will put his life on the line for me, no questions asked. And he is loyal to the point of destruction. Plus, the others, even the jerk Colt, have grown on me. I might not be sure if I want them to stick around here, but I damn sure don't want them hurt or mauled by hellhounds.

"Okay, so let's flush them out." I can tell Eric wants to argue before I even speak the words out loud, so I cut him off. "We are here to get Satanael. Who is not supposed to be here either if you have forgotten. I'm already banged up and pissed off. I'd rather deal with this now, instead of waiting for them to attack when it's convenient for them."

Eric growls but doesn't try to convince me otherwise. He knows I'm right, and no matter how much he would love for me to be away from any harm, he can't hide the thrill of the fight that is glittering in his eyes. My mate has a soft spot for me and does his best to be kind and make me happy, but he is a trouble maker. And he loves every second of it.

"I can help." Narsi hisses but doesn't move to get out of my arms, even burrowing his head further in my hair.

"I know how you feel," Eric tells the Trowe before shaking his head. "Damn, Haltija."

Chapter Eleven

Eric

Still shaken from the fact I didn't want to release the dagger back to Helena, I scan the open space around us, following the Haltija deeper into the warehouse. I've been in this damn place many times in the days I was waiting on my mate to agree and see her father. It was always empty, abandoned, apart from Satanael still held at the far back of it. Now, the stench of demons is fresh, making me grind my teeth. The jinn may not be something I'll happily face head on, but demons? I will rip the fuckers limb from limb just for daring to look her way.

Helena's hand lightly touches the middle of my back, her fingers cold and her palm damp. She is nervous. I can't blame her for disliking things connected to Hell, but I think this still has more to do with Satanael than the hellhounds. The air shifts around us, my skin tightening in a warning a second before the Haltija yelps to alert us.

Spinning around, I push out with my wings, scooping Helena in my arms and rolling us away. A wide shadow with six red eyes sails behind my back, missing us by an inch. Landing in a crouch, I tuck my mate between my arm and my right wing, despite her protests. I can barely even feel her elbow in my ribs.

A hellhound as giant as a human horse is staring me down, not far enough away from my mate for my liking. Three heads with gaping mouths full of razor sharp teeth and extended canines dripping acid down its fur are watching every twitch of my muscles. All of the heads dip low, the ears pinning back, eyes glowing like the fires from my realm are reaching through them to pull us in the pits of Hell. I keep my gaze locked on the middle head because that's the one controlling all of them.

"Eric, if you don't move your wing right now, I'll bite the shit out of your arm." Helena's muffled voice gets the Hellhound to zero in on the wing protecting her, and I'm grinding my teeth to a pulp.

The woman will definitely be the death of me.

I see the Haltija creeping up behind the hound just as a

menacing growl raises the hairs on my neck. Helena stops wiggling, her hand grabbing my arm so tightly I can feel her blunt nails denting my skin. Good, maybe now she'll stay quiet and let me deal with this before it hurts both of us enough that we can't stop it from dragging us wherever it was told to deliver us. I almost curse out loud when Narsi hides again behind a stack of crates. Heat almost burning my side explains the Haltija's reaction, and the breath gets stuck in my throat when a low growl comes from my left.

"Oh my God, there are two of them." Helena breathes, her words barely audible but loud enough for me to hear them.

Seeing that both hellhounds are about to pounce at once, I release my power, the tight control of the shadows around me snapping. Dark tendrils come to life, twisting and turning, reaching for whatever has my full attention. Two of the heads from the Hellhound facing me perk up at that, staring at the shadows as if confused. Whiney growl sounds echo from the hound on my left.

"Go back to where you came from. Your prey is not here." My body stiffens, expecting them to attack.

The middle head cocks to the side.

Pushing harder, I send the tendrils wrapping around its large hind legs, its claw-tipped paws scraping the floor when they touch its fur. Helena shifts uneasily under my wing, and her hand disappears from my arm. That worries me more than the two vicious beasts facing off with me. A big blob of acid drops on the floor, the sound of burning and sizzling accompanied by a horrendous stench searing my nostrils. Incredulity leaves me stunned when I feel my feathers shifting, and part of my mate's face pops out between them.

"Oh shit!" Helena's power bursts out, and it's like needles stabbing me all over the skin. "Holy shit!" She yanks her face back.

The ground shudders, sending the Hellhounds swaying and almost tripping over their own legs. Lifting to my full height, taking Helena with me, I stare them down, pushing harder on the shadows to trap them just long enough to move my mate away if they jump. The Hellhound facing me lowers all three of its heads again, and this time the growl is not a warning. It has had enough, and its pushing its curiosity away.

Time's up.

"Narsi, the front one is ours." I have no time to react when the meaning of those words slams into my brain.

Helena bursts from under my wing, her dagger blazing in her hand. The Haltija releases an awful shriek, making me cringe before it bolts from behind the crates and jumps on the back of the Hellhound, latching onto the middle head and clamping its teeth on one ear. The second hound from my left lunges for Helena, and I throw myself at it, taking us rolling away from my mate as I'm gripping it to hold it down.

My mate is slashing at a hellhound, calling him an ugly doggy right now, and I almost lose the hold I have on the beast. A laugh bursts through my lips, but sharp teeth pierce the place where my wing connects to my shoulder blades, making me roar. Paying more attention to Helena will cost me significantly and get us both killed.

"Stop messing with it, Eric. Just kill the damn thing!" As graceful as a dancer, she twists around the snapping jaws of the hound, slashing every part of it that she can reach. "I killed fucking jinn, so I'll be damned if I let this ugly doggy mess me up now!"

Her head barely reaches its shoulders.

Jerking my head to the side, I nail one of the heads of my own hound on the more massive horns, laughing at the crazy situation. The other two heads snap around my face, forcing me to pull back. When I push it away from my body, I see the left head is hanging limply, its eyes empty in its sockets. Helena's scream is like a knife in my chest. Whipping around, I see her stabbing the hound at the center of its forehead on the middle head, the skin on her left arm burnt from the dripping acid of its jaws. The Hellhound freezes for a split second, a soft whimper coming from its chest before dropping like a rock to the ground.

Turning to me, Helena grins, her smile turning to horror a second before acid burns my back and chest, and sharp teeth sink into my shoulder. Throwing my head back, I roar in pain, reaching back with my hand as my claws rake over the hound's face. It only tightens its jaw, its long canines breaking the bone.

With a battle scream, Helena sails in the air over my head at the same time as the Haltija shrieks, both of them jumping on the hound. The weight on my shoulder pulls me to the side, and I almost sag on my knees from the sudden release of the burden on it. The teeth are still buried in my skin, making the moment confusing as fuck. Craning my neck, my eyes widen when I see the muzzle still attached to my shoulder, but the rest of the head is missing. A heavy thump sounds behind me, and I slowly turn around to see the beast motionless on the floor.

"I have no idea why we didn't just kill them from the start." Huffing, Helena drops on her ass, breathing heavily. "What were you doing? Trying to hypnotize them?"

"They could've killed you." My gut clenches at the thought. "My job is to protect you first, deal with the threat later."

"To kill me, they need to get past this first." Lifting her hand, she stabs the dagger in the air at me. "Plus, I'm sure that freakish fire would've reared its head again." Shuddering, she blows out a breath. I stare at her stupefied, the jaw of the hound still clamped on my shoulder. "I don't like this place." Looking around, she grimaces, ignoring the body of the Hellhound a foot away from her. "It gives me the heebie jeebies. Can we just grab Satanael and get the hell out of here?"

I'm reminded once again why I'm crazy in love with this woman.

"She bested you, Shadow." The damn Haltija giggles crazily, wiggling its head at me, making Helena laugh.

I'm also reminded why I want to wring both their necks on a daily basis.

Chapter Twelve

Helena

*O*kay, so my heart is in my throat, my lungs are shriveled like a prune, and I'm even clenching my butt cheeks. Not even the abominations I was hunting looked as horrible or as scary as the hellhounds. Hiding how freaked out I am, I laugh when Narsi starts taunting Eric. Better to laugh than to scream from the top of my lungs and run like a coward.

"I think we should get out of here before something else jumps us." Pushing off the floor, I'm slow to remove my hand I have pressed on it. My knees are made out of jelly. "And good job Narsi." Smiling at my sidekick, I pet his head awkwardly. "You totally kicked some hellhound ass."

"Unlike Shadow." Snickering and giggling like he is deranged, he flips in circles like a dog chasing its tail.

Eric snarls.

"I think he has ADHD." After snatching air a few times, I finally grab Narsi's hair to stop him from moving. "It could also be his diet. Too many faces, maybe?"

"Haltijas are not pets, Hel." Pressing his lips in a firm line, Eric yanks out the dangling muzzle from his shoulder.

My heart skips a beat.

Remembering the last time he had a gaping hole in his body and didn't wake up for days, I rush to his side, dropping Narsi in the process. Slapping his hands away, I inspect his shoulder, pulling him down so I can see better. To my relief, the mauled part is rapidly healing as I watch.

"Okay…" Blowing out a relieved breath, I slap his still-bleeding shoulder harder than I want to, making him flinch. "You're going to be okay."

"You can *not* just jump at demonic creatures and expect me to be fine with it." Rounding on me, Eric snarls angrily.

Ignoring his tantrum, mostly because my knees are still knocking together from the fact that I saw two hellhounds staring me in the face, I look around. "If you haven't noticed, jumping at demonic creatures is the story of my life." Narsi is crawling on all fours sniffing at the dead hounds, and my stomach drops to my feet. He better not start eating them or I'll hurl right here where I'm standing. "And just to remind you, I'm jumping demonic creatures in more ways than one." Turning away from my sidekick, I wiggle my eyebrows at Eric. "On and off the field."

My comment takes him off guard, and after staring at me for a long moment, he shakes his head, unable to hide the smirk on his handsome face. My own lips twitch at that. As messed up at this whole thing is, I can genuinely say I got lucky in one thing. I couldn't find a better mate than Eric. For all his bullheadedness and arrogance, the prince of Hell is quite a catch, if I say so myself.

"This is the wrong place to be looking at me like that, Hel." Moving closer to where our skin is touching, his eyes project his own craving. "The worst place, I think."

"Right!" Snapping out of my lust-filled thoughts, I shift uncomfortably to eleviate the throbbing in my core. "It's the adrenaline talking, so don't let your ego blow up your head like a balloon." Grinning when he frowns, I slap his face a couple of times.

"Mistress." Narsi's hiss has us both moving.

Eric grumbles something that I can't quite catch as we hold our breaths to hear what got the Trowe's attention. Whoever has set up this trap strategically placed the crates around the vast, open space to be able to hide from view. It also gives us good coverage as to how we can flush them out and get rid of them. I watch Eric move his head around, his chin up, telling me he is trying to pinpoint the scent of whatever is lurking around us. My mind keeps going back to the placement of the large wooden boxes. Apart from being evil, heartless assholes, I may not know much about the jinn,, but this does not look like something they would do. So far, every encounter I've had with them has shown they love to show off, standing in plain sight because they think they are invincible. No, this is definitely not a jinn. I tell Eric as much while my eyes dart around, looking for a movement.

"No, it's not." He confirms my suspicion. "This stinks of Mammon from a mile away."

"So why are we crouching here? That asshole has been a thorn in my ass ever since we fought our way out of Hell. I really want to face him so I can shove my dagger up his nose." My fingers tighten on Eric's arm, where I'm leaning around it to peek at the dim area.

Narsi snickers from somewhere on our right.

"I don't like that he has brought hellhounds with him here, Hel." Turning his face around to look at me, I can see he wants to drag me out of here, kicking and screaming if he needs to. "We can come back with the others, and we should leave."

"Don't even think about it, Eric." Spitting the words at him, I tag on his arm for emphasis. "If you make me go back now, I'm never coming back here again."

Fine, it's a shitty move to threaten him with it, but I came here. I had to deal with that damn freaky fire coming out of me, and I saw my first hellhound. Like hell I'm going back now, especially when it will only give Mammon or whoever the asshole that set up this clusterfuck more time to plan. Eric's face is made out of granite, his lips whitening because he is pressing them together so hard.

"We came to get Satanael." Staring at him unblinking, I make sure he knows how serious I am. "We are getting Satanael, and leaving this damn place with him."

One jerky nod is my answer, but I'll take it. This stupid man will get himself killed, or let everyone else die so I don't get a scratch on me. It's getting old and annoying.

"Narsi, move to the front," Eric growls, finally looking away from my face.

My sidekick scurries from wherever he is hiding, and I release the breath I am holding under Eric's intent stare. Keeping my eyes on the back of the Trowe's head, I follow behind Eric as we get deeper into the warehouse. Reaching the far-right corner, we find a closed door that Narsi pushes open and disappears through. It's eerily silent around us, raising goosebumps over my arms. The tall ceilings make me feel like we are in a tomb, and the misty air only adds to it.

Eric leans on the wall, his head giving whatever is through the door a fast glance before repeating it again slowly. When there is no threat, he takes my hand and pulls us through it. The long hallway seems very familiar, and bile gathers at the back of my throat.

I've been here.

Memories drown me from the time when the Holy ass had me in his clutches. Windowless rooms, darkness, and shadows dancing around me. Needles poking my arms stealing my blood. This must be the first place the jinn pretending to be Michael kept me prisoner, before moving me to what we now call a safe house.

Cold sweat trickles down my back, and my hand gets slippery in Eric's palm. This must be one of the places I was held prisoner when the jinn disguised as Michael snatched me from the demon compound. My mate's hand tightens around my fingers, bringing me back from the panic attack that was about to overwhelm me.

"Hel?" My name is a whispered question, but I just nod at Eric, nudging him forward.

"I'm fine. Let's move." I'm also getting very good at lying. Amanda would've been proud.

We pass long, twisted hallways, closed, locked doors lining the walls on either side. Eric's hand is the only thing helping me to keep my shit together. Coming across a handful of giant demons that we dispatch too quickly for my liking helps keep the panic at bay also.

Narsi swivels his head like a bird when we reach a long stretch of flat, empty walls with just one metal door at the end of it. Looking back at Eric, my sidekick nods, his face set with determination. If that crazy little shit can keep it together, so can I.

We move faster, soundlessly stepping closer to the dead end where Narsi is already waiting, his arm stretched up, gripping the handle. As soon as we near him, he yanks on it, pulling it open and bolting through the darkness inside.

My heart lodges in my throat.

After what feels like an eternity, but it must be only precious seconds, Eric walks through the partly open door, pulling me behind him. I'm grateful that all I can see is his broad shoulders and beautiful black wings. He stands for a moment, then looking around and releasing my hand, he finally moves to the side, giving me a full view of the room. Everything in it disappears because my gaze latches onto green eyes so much like my own that it's like looking in a mirror.

"Satanael." His name is the breath leaving my lips.

Chapter Thirteen

Whatever I expect to feel when I finally meet my father, it is most definitely not this.

The man in front of me looks broken.

His sizable, muscled body hangs limply from the wall at the end of the small room where someone attached him to it with glowing metal chains, like a butterfly pinned to a display. His burgundy wings are stretched wide, taking up the span of the wall, looking broken in a few places. The pants are sticking to his massive thighs with dried-up blood that has leaked from his bare torso with hundreds of wounds on it. There is barely any clear skin left to see the skin tone. Blond hair just like my own is tangled on his head, falling over his slightly lifted face where those eyes are glued on me like I'm his lifeline. His body may be broken, but the fierce look in his gaze says he will rip anyone apart that dares to go anywhere near him.

"Shadow." Satanael's voice is deep and melodic, so full of pain that tears gather at the corners of my eyes.

"She came, Satanael." Eric does not move, standing stock still as if he doesn't want to spook him.

The man pinned like a painting on the wall.

"So, I see." Satanael does not look away from me, and I stand there like a rabbit caught in the gaze of the wolf ready to devour it whole. "Come closer, child."

My head jerks like I'm having a seizure, my hair flying around my face wildly when I can't speak to tell him no. I can't go closer even if I tried because my feet are nailed to the floor. A knowing smile lifts his dry mouth, and I watch a drip of blood slide down his chin when the skin splits at the center of his lower lip.

"My mistress does not fear you, Satanael." Narsi hisses from the side, jerking me out of the frozen state I was in. At least one of us has guts at the moment.

Eric snorts.

Satanael chuckles, his head dropping down on his chest.

"No, she does not," my father says softly, his words slightly muffled for the mass of hair that fell over his head. "She fears what her father makes her."

"You have no right to call yourself my father." I finally find my voice, but I sound more like a hurt child than the badass I should be.

"We don't have time for this conversation now," Eric chirps from where he is still standing like a statue. "We can talk back at the safe house. Mammon has his lackeys infesting the building. I doubt he will let us walk out of here easily."

"Good." Satanael groans, his body shuddering with pain or exhaustion, maybe both. "He and I have unfinished business."

"Dude, you can barely keep your eyes open." Blurting it out, I squeeze my eyes tightly shut. Really, this is ridiculous, and I'm acting like an idiot.

"Free me." Ignoring my outburst, my father's words are soft like a plea.

Confused, I turn to look at Eric. "What?"

"He didn't want to leave this place before he saw you. He didn't believe us that you are waiting in the safe house." Clenching his jaw, Eric glares at the top of Satanael's head. "Beelzebub ignored him, of course, and tried to rip the chains. He couldn't, and it seeped his strength like a sponge, almost killing him."

"What?" I sound like a parrot, but I'm confused as hell. What the hell do they want me to do exactly?

Eric looks pointedly at the dagger holstered on my thigh.

My heart gives my ribs a hard, painful thump.

Eric's face, the longing in his eyes when he held the dagger in front of the warehouse, floats to the front of my mind's eye. He released it, although reluctantly, and I like to think it was because he loves me more than he loves power. What will happen if the dagger gets in Satanael's hand? In the Devil's hand. Will he try to take it from me? Will I be able to stop him if he does?

"She doesn't trust me." My father sounds sad, and anger rears its head in my chest.

"You don't fucking say, Devil!" Sneering at the top of his head, guilt shuts me up the second the words leave my mouth. Trying to mask it, I turn to Eric. "If it almost killed Beelzebub, how is Satanael still alive?"

Okay, I have trust issues. But can you blame me?

"They are not warded to kill me." A deep sigh comes from my father. "Just to kill whoever tries to remove them." His head lifts slowly, only his intent eyes visible through the mess of hair over his face. "They did that after they brought you in this building, thinking if you knew I was here, you will do everything to come to me; to free me. They wanted you dead if that was the case."

The confirmation that I was, in fact, held here is like a blow to my head. I guess deep down I was hoping that I'm wrong about that. The ground shudders under our feet violently. I sway on my feet, and Eric moves for the first time, snatching me by the arm so I don't drop like a rock. Satanael growls, a chilling sound that curdles the blood in my veins. My mate ignores him, looking down at me with concern etched on his face. Narsi hisses something that I can't hear.

"Hel?" Pulling me to his chest, he cups my face with his other hand. "I will kill anyone that tries to touch, and you know that."

"I know." Swallowing thickly, I take a deep, slow breath, Eric's nearness calming me down. "I know." Repeating it helps me compose myself better.

"I see." Satanael is still watching me, my gaze connecting with his when I turn to look at him.

"Good for you." Now that I know the jinn had me here, I want to leave faster than I can blink. "How exactly do you want me to do this?"

"I think you can cut the chains with the dagger," Eric answers my question.

"He can't stand." Eyeing my father warily, I doubt we will get out of here alive if Eric has to drag his ass.

"I'll be able to walk on my own when the chains are gone." It's crazy how much the stubborn lift of his chin resembles mine. I push that thought aside because I'll leave him here if I keep thinking about it.

"Good, because if you can't, I'm not letting Eric die for you. I'll kill you myself before he gets hurt on your behalf." Pushing off Eric, I look at the chains closely. "I'm surprised no one has come to stop us." My offhanded comment makes Eric jerk back.

"Oh, they'll try." Rolling his shoulders, he reaches his arm to his back, squeezing the spot where the hellhound bit him. "They'll wait for us when we try to leave. The room is too small. Anyone that tries to walk in will die before one foot is through it."

"Right." My words sound distracted because I can't find what's holding the chains to the wall. "So I just slash them wherever? It doesn't matter the spot, right?" My fingers tighten on the hilt as I pull the dagger out.

Satanael's gaze snaps to it in an instant.

"Don't even think about it!" Waving it at him, I glare. "I'll cut you the second you try to go anywhere near it."

Satanael chuckles.

Humor dances in his eyes as he looks at me with some emotion that I'm unwilling to name. My stomach clenches, and my chest feels tight.

"You are so much like your mother," my father says softly, and I want to burst out crying. Tears overflow my eyes, and somehow, I blink them away.

Get your shit together, Hel! yelling at myself internally, I ignore Satanael.

"Okay, I'll cut, and you grab him if he topples over." Rolling my neck, you'd think I'm about to fight a horde of demons.

"I got him." Eric moves with me as I approach my father. "And, Hel." His hand grabs my upper arm, stopping me for a moment. "If you feel even a second of weakness, you step away. Do you hear me?"

I nod, still looking at the chains. My dagger starts glowing slightly, the colors dancing around us and all over Satanael's body. It lights up all his injuries and a lump forms in my throat. There is no way he will be able to move without help. I'm not even sure how he is still alive.

"I will be fine when you remove them, child." My father sounds like he is reassuring me, obviously noticing my worry.

I glare at him.

"I don't care." My angry words only make him smile, knowingly pissing me off more. "Let's do this."

That smile was enough to freak me out. Not wanting to stand here anymore and deal with the hundreds of emotions swirling inside me, I slash out wildly at the metal links surrounding my father. As soon as my dagger touches the chain, a bright light bursts from the contact, blinding me for a second. Turning my head away, I put more pressure on it, and I feel the blade separating the links. A blast of air sends me crashing to the opposite wall before I drop on my ass. Stunned, I look up, blinking the bright spots from my vision.

The chains are all piled up on the floor.

Satanael is on all fours, his wings draping limply on either side of him. Eric is lifting himself off the floor at my right, and Narsi is shaking his head, having flown close to me in the blast. My jaw hangs open as I watch the dark red appendages crack and jerk as they straighten themselves up. Satanael is healing as I watch, faster than anyone I've ever seen.

His head lifts, and he smiles at me.

My stomach drops to my feet.

"Thank you, child." He lifts himself up, shaking off the wings before they snap close to his back. "Let us get out of here."

Chapter Fourteen

*E*ric opens the door, sticking his head out for a second before nodding to Narsi. The Trowe practically flies out of the room, not giving me time to stop him. When Satanael moves to walk out, my mate grips his shoulder, stopping him, and some communication passes between them as they wordlessly stare at each other.

It pisses me off.

"Keep the bromance to a minimum, you two. I want to get out of here." Bristling, I shoulder my way between them, following my sidekick.

The hallways are empty as I inch through them, but there is expectancy thrumming in the air around me that I can't shake off. I'm not sure if it's coming from me, or if it's coming from bodies in the shadows waiting for their first chance to jump on us. Eric's wing brushes my arm when he gets himself in front of me, but I don't miss the annoyance plastered on his face that tells me he is not happy I just left them staring at each other back there. Luckily, we are trying to get out of here without too much trouble, or I would've had a lot to say to his stubborn ass about that.

"I'm not sure I like him at my back." Walking faster, so I'm closer to Eric, I murmur under my breath in hopes Satanael doesn't hear me.

He does, obviously, his chuckle confirming it.

"Helena, please. Let's get out of here first. He won't do anything to hurt you."

Taken aback, I clamp my mouth shut, clutching the dagger in a white-knuckled grip. Eric says my full name only when he wants to strangle me because I'm doing something stupid according to him, or when he is afraid for my life. My comment inside this warehouse counts as two for one, I guess.

We pause at a junction, anxiety eating a hole in my stomach when I can't even hear Narsi nearby. The stupid thing is dumb enough to get himself killed when he thinks I've trusted him with a mission. Eric has been taking advantage of that lately, and I make a mental note to remember to talk to him about it when we get to the safe house. No one may care about Narsi, and I can't say he is not a little disturbing, but he is under my skin. I care.

"I can't hear Narsi." Holding onto Eric's arm, I lean over him to peek around the corner.

"The damn Haltija is fine." Yanking me back, Eric scowls at me.

I elbow him in the ribs for being a jerk.

"You have not told my daughter much about Haltija's, I presume?" Satanael mumbles softly from behind me.

Turning to look at him, I startle again at our resemblance. We don't look alike per se. It's more the subtle tells of mannerism along with the same color hair and eyes that make me feel uneasy. Like watching him now with a determined look on his face. I've seen that look many times in the mirror.

"Come on." Eric moves, and it breaks the perusal I have on my father.

"It shouldn't be this quiet." Keeping a hand on Eric's back, I follow close on his heels. "I don't like it."

"It's quiet because they are only brave when magical chains hold me down." Satanael's voice booms around us, echoing from down the hallway too.

I almost swallow my tongue.

"What the hell are you doing?" Hissing at him, the ground shudders, reacting to my panic.

"I grow tired of slinking around like vermin when it's them that need to fear for their pathetic lives." Squaring his shoulders, my father struts down the hallway like he owns the place, leaving me gaping at his back.

"Satanael…" Eric growls in warning, his nostrils flaring in anger, and the muscle in his jaw is doing an impressive tap dance.

"What happened to you, Shadow?" Turning around and walking backward, my father grins at Eric. "Have they made you forget who you are?"

"I know very well who I am." Shadows jump around us, flaring to life with Eric's anger. "I also have a mate that I don't want to see hurt."

"There are no jinn here." Dismissing him, Satanael flips around and continues walking. "Whoever is here should hide from us, not the other way around."

"This is why he was chained to a wall." Hurrying after Eric, I grind my teeth. "The dumbass is so arrogant he will get us all killed. I should've left him back there."

"Did she just call me a dumbass?" Satanael finally stops walking, and we almost slam into his back.

"I did." If looks could kill, my father would've been dead by now from the anger burning my eyes at the moment.

"She is your daughter," Eric says dryly, and I turn my gaze on him, making him flinch.

"I didn't hear you complaining until now." Still glaring at Eric, I'm doing my best not to let my anger and fear bring the warehouse down on top of our heads.

The air around us gets thicker with tension, and it's

not coming from the three of us. At my words, Eric looks pointedly at Satanael, as if I just proved his point or something. My hand is itching to slap his handsome face. My father throws his head back, a burst of deep belly laughter bending him back before his head snaps up, and those bright eyes lock on my face.

"She's perfect!" Something akin to a pride twinkles in his gaze, twisting my stomach into knots.

"Yes, yes, she is." Eric smiles gently at me.

"You do realize that's not a compliment coming from the two you, right?" Speaking slowly like they have difficulties understanding, I look from one to the other. "Lucifer's son"—Stabbing my finger at Eric first, I turn it to my father next—"and the Devil."

"Where did Zadkiel hide her exactly all these years?" All the humor is gone and Satanael's face gets clouded in anger, sending a shiver down my spine.

"That's a long story." Having done enough chatting, Eric takes my hand, passing by Satanael and dragging me along with him. I'm stunned enough by the sudden shift in personality that I follow along, my neck twisting so I can keep my eyes on my father. "You'll hear all about it when we are not in the middle of a horde of demons."

"Yes." Still holding me pinned under his intent gaze, Satanael follows behind us with a frown. "I'm looking forward to hearing that story."

"I bet you are." Murmuring under my breath, I release a deep sigh when I finally look away from him.

"Keep your head in the game, Hel." Chuckling, Eric glances over his shoulder at me since I'm dragging my feet. "You are just as cocky as your father, but there might be hundreds of them waiting for us out there. I need you unharmed."

"I'm not…"

"She will be unharmed. I will kill them all myself." Slicing a hand in the air, Satanael rolls his shoulders, cutting me off before I declare I'm not like him.

I'm reminded of all the times I've jumped in a fight to try and do precisely that, ensuring no one else gets hurt. Eric is watching me with a pointed look in his eyes, and my mouth twists in frustration.

"I see your point." I sound dejected, making Eric laugh, and the smile brightens his face.

We are almost at the vast open space where we entered the warehouse while they both chuckle, annoying the hell out of me. Determined to prove them wrong, I set my mind on keeping my mouth shut and my anger to a minimum. Just like everyone keeps reminding me, I have angel blood in my veins, too. How hard would it be to act angelic? Raphael's face comes to mind, his kind, soft voice and compassionate gaze warming up my chest just thinking about it.

I can so do that! I tell myself a second before Eric yanks on my arm, shoving me behind his broad shoulders. Satanael crowds closer, placing me sandwiched between two large men and no idea on what's going on.

"Mammon said no one leaves this place alive," a voice from nightmares speaks from somewhere in front of us.

Power slams me from the front and back, Eric and Satanael both seemingly growing in size as the anger turns to a tangible thing in the air. That strange energy surges through me, the dagger in my hand blazing with bright colors in reaction to the aggression surrounding me. My skin stretches thin, trying to contain it, almost making me cry out in pain. My father places a hand on my shoulder, touching me for the first time. The pain dissipates to a slight burn, and I release a breath in relief.

"Better?" Satanael asks softly, concern evident in his voice from a mile away. I don't acknowledge it, pretending I don't hear it.

"Yes." Not ready to thank him yet, I wiggle my shoulder to remove his hand.

"Satanael." Narsi pops out of nowhere, hissing loudly. "There are twice as many outside." My sidekick squeezes between all of us, latching onto my leg.

"Hel?" Eric says my name like a question, and I'm grateful he is making sure that I'm ready for whatever we are facing instead of trying to shove me in a corner to hide me. My mate is either learning, or having my father here makes him more confident about our chances of getting out of here alive. It rubs me wrong, but I don't have time for that now. I want to get out of here as much as they do.

"Let's do this." Cracking my neck, I shake my leg to tell Narsi to let go.

The Trowe chuckles creepily with glee, dropping on all fours. His mouth stretches wide, the rows of yellowed teeth bared in a hellish mockery of a smile. Another reminder that I'm kind of glad he is on our side if I'm honest with myself.

Eric and Satanael move at the same time, positioning themselves on either side of me, giving me my first look at what we are facing. Standing just a couple of feet inside the front, open area of the warehouse, the three of us, with Narsi crouched at my feet, are looking at a few dozen demons spread out. Well, we are looking. My sidekick has his eyeless sockets trained in that direction. Most of them are on the ground, claws ready to tear us apart. The rest are on top of the stacked-up crates, looking from above, waiting to pounce when we are too busy fighting. I look at Narsi, who's been focused on me like a hawk. His mouth stretches wider at my unspoken command.

"I'll eat their face." Hissing happily, he bolts at the first pile of crates, climbing it like a monkey.

My own smile blooms on my face as I twirl my dagger. "Playtime, motherfuckers!"

"She is perfect!" Satanael chuckles, reminding me I screwed up and all hopes of being angelic disappear down the drain.

"Oh, well…" I blow out a breath before the demons swarm us.

Chapter Fifteen

Eric

The fucker I'm fighting almost takes half of my wing off while I gawk at Helena. Twisting away with a groan, I shove my claws under his chin, lifting him off his feet. The grip he had on my wing disappears as I dangle him harshly before flipping him away like a rag doll. They jumped at us all at once, but after a short time, they realized their mistake. Mammon sent strong demons to stop us from leaving, but I'm pretty sure he didn't expect Satanael to be with us. The arrogant fool thought the chains would stop Helena. There is no doubt in my mind that the jinn didn't share everything with him after this.

With the first wave, half of the demons are scattered in pieces around us, leaving the rest debating if they should continue fighting or run. Mammon must be holding something over their heads if they are still here with the show Helena and Satanael are giving them as I watch. The two of them don't even need me to fight. I can just stand behind and pick off those stupid enough to try to attack from the back.

Satanael is a whirlwind of red wings and claws, all his rage at being held helpless so long coming out in the merciless beheading and maiming of everything within reach. At first, he went at them mindless and blind with wrath. The moment Helena nears him, his movements become more calculated, even though I can see he is not thinking straight. Something primal in him recognizes his blood, and he is twisting around her without touching, turning their collective battle into a sight to behold.

Helena grins as her glowing dagger splits a demon in half, her long hair flying around her face when she spins, kicking her leg above her head and nailing the next beast in the throat. Satanael slides under her leg, an impressive feat for a large male like himself, his claws ripping the chest of another foe coming from their right. I feel the air stir around me, and my hand shoots out, grabbing a demon by the throat. The moron thinks I'm too distracted to notice him inching closer. He must not have seen the shadows guiding his feet to me. It just adds more stupidity on Mammon's part. Where did he find these mindless fools to follow his lead?

"Eric, are you getting a tan over there?" Helena huffs before jumping, jamming her dagger between the eyebrows of a demon twice her size. "A little help will be nice." Dangling, holding the hilt in a tight grip, she goes down when the demon drops, rolling off him before pouncing on her feet.

"You don't look like you need help, cupcake." Smirking at her, I jerk my chin, pointing at Satanael.

Her mouth flattens in a thin line, and she gives me a side-eye glance, making me chuckle. Satanael looks distractedly at us before grinning wide at his daughter. His right wing spreads out fast, slapping the demon running at him, sending the idiot flying through the wall. He takes one of the crates with him as well, the force of the hit making a large hole wide enough to give us a glimpse of the street. Only two demons are left inside the warehouse with us, both perched on top of crates, one dropping on the ground with half of his face missing.

The Haltija pops his head out from above Helena, a broad grin on his blood-smeared face. "One more, Shadow!" Hissing at me, he jumps down, scurrying at the pile with the last foe watching all of us in horror.

The stench of blood is searing my nostrils when I look around, making sure no one else is lurking hidden behind the piles of wooden chests. Satanael's power spreads about like probing fingers doing precisely the same, and I see Helena shiver, staring at me wide eyed.

"He can sense them better." Waving her concern away, I stride to my mate. "Satanael feels their anger like it's his own. I'm sure he can pin point where all of them are, even the ones outside by now."

"Right." Helena purses her lips, blowing out a deep breath, and my eyes lock on her mouth. A smile tilts the corners of her lips when she notices my distraction. "Maybe we should get this over with faster." Her voice lowers, the words breathy, raising goosebumps on my arms. My pants are tight as we keep our gazes locked.

"I do not need to watch this!" Groaning, Satanael closes his eyes as if pained.

My mouth opens, the need to apologize to the male for eye fucking his daughter in front of his eyes dying on my tongue when Helena slaps a hand on her hip. Instead of an apology, a grin spreads my mouth so wide my face hurts. It looks like the unease and shock my mate felt about her father is wearing off, and Satanael is about to get his first tongue lashing. I'm going to enjoy this so much it should be illegal.

"Then go fucking home, asshole!" Glaring at him, Helena waves her dagger threateningly at her father. "This"—Pointing between her and me, her hip juts out —"does not concern you."

"I am your father." Frowning at her, Satanael's

shoulders snap back. "Everything to do with you concerns me."

"You are twenty years too late." Helena is angry, but she can't hide the hurt in her words from me. My gut clenches at that, making me growl at Satanael.

"You can feel the bond, Satanael. So, stop the bullshit." Pulling Helena under my arm, I curl my wing protectively around her shoulder. "There is much to be said, and we can't do it here. I have a feeling they have a few hellhounds out there, as well. There is no way Mammon had only two waiting on us."

"I'm not sure I want to hear all of it." Shoulders slumping, Satanael rubs a hand over his face. "When you live as long as I have, twenty years is just a blink of an eye. To me, you are still the babe I saw taken away swaddled in a blanket."

Helena trembles in my arms and I glare at the male, pushing the words through clenched teeth. "As I said, now is not the time."

"Why is Lucifer not here?" Satanael changes the subject so abruptly I just blink at him a few times before understanding what he is saying.

"Because he was as stupid as you and got caught," Helena blurts out, still unsettled by the conversation. "They have Michael, too. Also, they tried to capture Raphael, but we got lucky and stopped them."

Satanael's eyes narrow slightly, I can see his mind racing with the bits and pieces he is picking up from us.

His mouth purses, reminding me of Helena when she is deep in thought. She would've been biting on her nails too. Smiling at her, I look down at her face.

"You ready to kick some ass and get out of here?" Kissing her forehead, I'm rewarded with a sigh and the relaxing of her stiff shoulders. "Maybe Raphael is back by now with some good news, too." I realize my mistake, stiffening, as soon as the words leave my mouth.

"You are working with the Archangels?" The anger I was expecting does not come, so I relax my shoulders before turning to Satanael. "Raphael is helping you?"

"He is, and if you have a problem with that, you should just stay here." Helena gets defensive of Raphael, as I expected.

"Why would I have a problem that your destiny is unfolding, child?" A slight smile softens the harshness on Satanael's face. "Let us go see if the white-feathered ass is back. I have words for him."

With that bomb, Satanael turns towards the front double doors, pushing them open with a flourish as he strides outside where hordes of demons are lying in wait. Helena and I glance at each other. She shrugs a shoulder, apparently deciding to ignore that last statement before she moves to follow her father. My feet track my mate, that invisible cord tying us together, tugging at the center of my chest. I barely notice the Haltija scampering past me to follow his mistress.

Chapter Sixteen

Helena

"I'm wondering if we should've left him chained." Pressing my back to Eric's, I slash out wildly with the dagger. "This literally looks like we unleashed the Devil."

Eric grunts, not saying a word. *Accidentally,* which is not by accident at all, I shove my elbow between his ribs. He flinches away, and the grunt this time holds more pain. From me and from the demon that got a good hit while Eric was distracted.

"Don't you dare ignore me, Eric!" Kicking out, my

boot connects with the demon's chest, sending him stumbling back into the two others waiting their turn.

"I'm not ignoring you, Hel." The sound of skin hitting skin in rapid succession stalls his words, but he continues talking as soon as the demon he was punching drops. "I just don't know what you want me to say without you getting upset with me. If you tell me, it'll be much easier."

Giggling like an idiot, I'm awarded with a roar when I slice off a demon's arm at the wrist, the claws scraping the pavement when it hits the ground. "Oh my God! I'm not that bad!"

"Okay."

With that agreement, Eric moves away from fighting his own bunch of idiots that decided to stick around us. Everyone else is too busy trying to stop my father. Satanael went a little nuts the second he recognized some of the demons that used to be loyal to him at some point. Apparently, that was a big no-no, and they should've known better. Looking at him plowing through them like an elephant in a glass house, I must agree with that.

They really shouldn't have stabbed him in the back.

Knowing all too well how betrayal feels, I can't say I blame him. Although, in my case, I feel worthless, like something is wrong with me for those close to me to do that. Not my father. He took that as a free pass to turn them into a lump of minced meat, going further and even stomping on whatever was left of them. A shudder rakes my bones as I watch it all from the corner of my eye.

Maybe the demons fighting Eric and I are not stupid, but the smartest of the group. Satanael is on my side, and I don't want to be anywhere near him right now.

Eric, on the other hand, is a different story.

"What the hell is the matter with you, monster boy? Last time I checked; I didn't burn your balls off earlier tonight. You still have them, right?" Glancing to confirm he is listening; I see him glaring at me. "What? What's with the okay?"

His eyes flick to where my father is tossing a demon, holding him by the feet and slamming his head left and right. "I'd rather you weren't upset while Satanael is pissed off."

I almost lose an eye when his words stop me suddenly. The demon scratches the crap out of my face, but luckily, he doesn't blind me. Eric shoots like an arrow, nailing him in his horns, throwing the demon a few feet away. Narsi bolts after it, no doubt to eat his face because my sidekick is like a bottomless pit.

"You are scared of my father." My words are as flat as ever.

"You aren't?" One of Eric's eyebrows lifts up, daring me to say no.

"Right."

Looking around, I realize we have no more demons to fight. The one that got his hand chopped off is running away, the heels of his boots hitting his ass as he disappears from view.

"As I said"—Squatting down, I start cleaning the blood off my dagger on the pants of the dead demon closest to me—"maybe we should've left him chained up. I'm not sure how long the jinn had him, but maybe he is…" Not wanting to say it out loud in case he can hear me, I twirl a finger around my ear while looking up at Eric.

Frowning, Eric turns to watch Satanael with a thoughtful expression. My stomach does a summersault, the familiar fear that somehow I doom humanity because I act before I think rearing its head with a vengeance. What the hell is wrong with me? I need to stop acting like an idiot before it's too late for all of us.

"He is not." Eric's voice jolts me out of the downward spiral I was headed towards head-first.

"What?" Still crouched, my neck hurts from having my face tilted all the way up to look at him.

"He is not…" Following my example, Eric twirls his finger around his ear, his claw catching on his tousled hair and almost yanking a chunk of it off. "For fuck's sake." Growling, he tugs on it harder.

Bursting out laughing, I lift myself up and grab his forearm to stop him from ripping his hair off. "Stop." He struggles for a moment, and I slap the dagger I'm holding on his shoulder, freezing him in an instant. "Stop pulling, would ya?"

"This is what you do to me." His eyes are blazing, burning holes on my face while I'm untangling his hair from the sharp-tipped claw. "I forget what and who I am around you."

"Is that a bad thing?" My heart is hammering in my chest.

I know Eric loves me. He is even stubborn enough to die just to prove that on a daily basis. But that fear from having everyone I love stabbing me in the back does not want to rest. Does having Satanael free mean that Eric doesn't feel the need to be around me now? Was protecting me his only motivation to be with me? I accepted the fact we are mates, but that doesn't mean I truly understand it. As far as I know, he can turn his back at any moment, leaving and never coming back. Is that what he is saying now? Does it bother him how much he has changed being with me? Will he decide to walk away because of that? He never wanted a commitment in the first place. My fingers tremble as I gently pull the twisted hair apart.

"Hel, look at me." Eric's voice is soft, the murmured words like a clap of distant thunder in his chest. "Hey, I said look at me." Using his free hand, he crooks a finger under my chin, turning my face towards him. "What's going on in that pretty head of yours?"

Locking my gaze on his, I can't stop the tears overflowing my eyes. I'm such a mess with the anxiety of seeing my father, freeing him, fighting hellhounds, and what have you, that this is just like a cherry on top of the cake. One treacherous tear escapes, trickling down my face. Eric's eyes widen, the blood draining from his face.

"Helena?" My name is just the breath passing his lips.

"Do you want to leave now?" Blurting it out, I flinch when my voice cracks. "We freed my father," I add as an explanation to exactly nothing.

"What?" Taking a step back as if I slapped him, Eric stares at me in shock. My hand drops limply at my side when he pulls away from me.

Another tear rolls from my eye, making a wet trail on the side of my nose before sliding over my lips until I taste its salty flavor on my tongue.

"You said that you don't feel like yourself…"

"Are you insane?" Eric doesn't let me finish, his body returning to his human form as he yanks me to his chest. "I will destroy the worlds if they try to take you from me, Hel." Cupping my face between his palms, Eric's face blurs when I let myself cry. "You are mine, Helena. Not the jinn, not my father, and most definitely not your father will ever change that."

Burying my face in his neck, I wrap my arms around him. I must've freaked him out a lot because he doesn't bat an eye that I still have the dagger in one of my hands. My body shakes with my sobs, and I feel Eric trembling as well.

"But you said…"

"I'm a fool, Helena." Snarling angrily, he tightens his arms around me so much I can barely take a breath.

"Haven't you learned that by now. What I meant was I can't think straight when I'm around you. Because I love you, and I will go crazy if you get hurt." Pushing his face in my hair, his voice breaks, "I love you. Don't you know that it scares me just how much I love you?"

"I love you, too." My sobs turn to sniffles as I hold onto him for dear life. "I love you the same."

"I have no idea why you dragged me here." A voice I didn't expect to hear jerks Eric and me apart. "They don't need help. They're humping like rabbits in the middle of the street."

Chapter Seventeen

"Seriously, Colt? Do you always have to be an asshole?" I wipe my face, hoping the jerk can't see that I've been crying.

Colt is standing next to Beelzebub, both of them with their arms folded over their chest. Beelzebub moves, slapping Colt in the back of the head, glaring at Eric's twin with his red eyes.

"They were having a moment." The massive fallen snarls at Colt.

"We already know the she devil has my brother by the balls. I'm embarrassed for him most of the time." Rubbing at his head, Colt winks at me, taking the sting off his mean words.

"You really are a jerk." But his words did what he intended, my lips twitching while I'm suppressing a smile.

"I see Satanael is out and about."

Beelzebub tilts his chin at my father, who is down to one demon and is taking his time with him. It looks like he is ripping his claws one by one. Shuddering, I turn away from the grisly sight.

"You know him for a long time, right?" Looking at Beelzebub, I stare at him intently in case he tries to lie to me. "Does he look normal to you? I mean, he is not nuts, right? Because captivity and torture can turn anyone insane, I think…" Closing my mouth with an audible snap, I stop blubbering like an idiot.

Beelzebub looks confused, so he turns to Eric for a translation of my onslaught of questions. You'd think I was speaking Swahili, not English. Colt is grinning like a loon the whole time, that left eye winking like the broken blinker of a car.

"Satanael is righting a wrong. Many of Mammon's lackeys were once loyal to him, apparently." My mate translates on a sigh.

"Ah!" Beelzebub nods in understanding.

"I ate their face." Narsi hisses proudly, puffing out his narrow chest.

"Someone, kill the Haltija, please." Colt turns hopefully, first to Eric then to Beelzebub. When both of them just glare at him, he eyes my father thoughtfully.

"Don't even think about it, Colt. I'll gut you like a fish." I take a step towards him, but Eric pulls me back.

Narsi giggles, wiggling at Colt, taunting him. Grabbing his hair, I pull him to my side, and he latches onto my leg the same second. The crunching of footsteps turns my head so I can look over my shoulder. The breath gets stuck in my throat, and I'm lucky the eyes don't pop out of my sockets.

My father is sauntering towards us in the middle of the street. He is covered in demon blood from head to toe, the wings rustling on his back, shaking off blood drops like a dog shaking off water from its fur. His right hand is wiping off his bare torso, but more like smearing the crimson over it than doing anything else. His gaze flicks to everyone but stays honed-in on my face, and he grimaces from what I assume is horror written all over it.

"I did not wish for you to see that." It's the first thing he says to me when he stops at our circle. "Beelzebub." Nodding once at the fallen, he turns and frowns at Eric's twin. "Colt, I never thought I'd see you here."

"Lots of firsts lately, Satanael." Unbothered, Colt is still grinning so much you'd think he is on something.

"Indeed." My father nods thoughtfully, which looks absolutely ridiculous when he is covered in blood.

"You left George and Cass alone in a house full of hunters after my friends made it clear that they are on our side?" Remembering what bothered me when I saw Colt and Beelzebub here, panic bubbles in my chest. "If anything happens to them, I'll pull your wings off."

"I'll help her." Satanael nods once, shocking all of us into silence. "What? Hunters are bad news; we know this!" His eyes squint at us in suspicion. "What am I missing here?"

Eric groans, covering his face with a hand. Colt's grin grows even more, if that's possible.

"I am a hunter." Turning to fully face him, I crane my neck to stare at him.

Satanael jerks back like I just stabbed him, his eyes turning comically round on his blood-covered face. His gaze flicks from Eric to Beelzebub, then to Colt before settling back on me.

"No," he breathes.

"Yes." Nodding slowly, I keep an eye on his shoulders in case he decides to attack. You never know after a reaction like that.

"Well, technically she's not a hunter anymore," Colt chirps, enjoying the situation a hell of a lot more than is good for him. "Not after they hired a hit on her head."

Now I really think that Satanael's eyes are about to pop out and roll down the street.

"It was that Holy ass that made all the trouble, asshole." Glaring at Colt, I clench my teeth, grinding the words out. "My father tried to keep me safe by placing Eric in my path." As soon as I said the words, my entire body freezes. Even the blood stops pumping through my veins.

Three sets of eyes snapped at Satanael's face, Colt's grin slipping like it never existed, Eric shifts to his demonic form, with Beelzebub going a step further by pulling me slowly away from Eric and pushing me behind his back. Even Narsi straightens up, stepping closer to Eric in solidarity.

"Her father…" Satanael says so softly the short hairs on the back of my neck stand on end.

"Until I found her, Helena didn't know who or what she was." Eric's deep voice does not calm me like it usually does. "She was told she is a human orphan blessed by Heaven to be a hunter for the Order."

"You take me for a fool, Shadow?" I jump a foot of the ground when Satanael roars. "You are telling me the Order will not know a hybrid is under their roof?"

"The one she thought was her father must've shielded her. My suspicion is through a brew or something while she was younger. When she became of age, I believe it was in the weapons he gifted her."

My head pops out from behind Beelzebub to stare at Eric. What the hell is he talking about? This is the first time he has said anything like this. Not that we've had a lot of time to talk things through, but I would think something like this is important enough to be pointed out.

Eric does not look away from Satanael.

"Where is Zadkiel?" My father looks at me, and my

heart lodges in my throat at the emptiness in his stare. I open my mouth to tell him she's dead.

"We don't know," Beelzebub says evenly, his large palm sneaking out, pushing me behind him again. I glare at his back.

"There is much we need to discuss, and standing here is not the right place to do it." Eric does have a point. I glance around as much as I can, seeing the bodies of the demons already disappearing from sight.

"Step away from my daughter." Beelzebub stiffens his wings, snapping out at the aggression in Satanael's voice.

"I'm stepping out." Yelping louder than was necessary, I jump into motion. "The daughter is stepping out, so let's just all calm down. No need to get violent." Colt snorts but I ignore his ass. I'll deal with him later. "Jesus, you guys are really intense. What the hell?"

Eric presses the bridge of his nose with a thumb and a forefinger, and for a second, I wonder how he doesn't poke his eyes out with those claws. I guess I'm giving him enough of a headache that he is willing to push his luck. Some of the liveliness returns in Satanael's gaze, his eyes twinkling in humor until I realize I just called out God's name while standing with three creatures from Hell. One of them the Devil, nonetheless.

Clearing my throat, I look at my father sheepishly. "I mean, gee…" Colt chuckles louder, so I turn to glare at him. "You, I can stab without blinking an eye."

Eric does not remove the hand from his face. Poor guy.

"Let's go home. We can talk there." Beelzebub turns on his heels, striding down the street without looking if we will follow. The word home clenches my stomach tightly.

One by one, we move as well, Eric and I taking the rear with Narsi jumping crazily around us. Releasing a sigh, Eric takes my hand, having returned to his human form thankfully. He gives my fingers a reassuring squeeze, and I cling to his hand like a lifeline. The first rays of dawn crest over the sky, lightening it. I have a feeling it'll be a long day, and an even longer time until I get to sleep for a bit.

Chapter Eighteen

"We didn't think this through." I'm watching our safe house warily, standing a couple of feet away from the wards.

"No, we didn't." Eric looks as flustered as I feel.

Since the SUV was a lost cause, we had to walk through the streets of Atlanta to get back here. The sun is already high in the sky, and as bad as it sounds, I'm glad there are no humans around. Eric, Satanael, and I are covered in blood and gore like some actors from a horror movie. The difference is, our crap is real.

Watching Satanael breathing heavily to control his anger while he glares at the safe house, my mind goes back to the couple of humans we found walking the streets. Dressed in military uniforms, they patrolled the area of downtown Atlanta. Curiosity got the better of me, so I bolted when Eric tried to stop me and interrogated the shit out of them. They may have not been willing to share anything with me but seeing the three large males plus my wing adorned father convinced them to sing like canaries. One of them even fainted when he saw Narsi. I do feel bad for that one.

Releasing a deep breath, my shoulders relax a little. What they told me made me feel slightly better, although it's not much. Apparently, when the gate of Hell opened, and the jinn started wrecking chaos, the humans managed to border out Atlanta, keeping this clusterfuck centered here instead of spreading everywhere. Eric pointed out that the humans must've had help from a magic user or an Archangel. We're just not sure about that, and the humans had no clue. What they did sound very proud of was the fact that it was effortless to keep this nightmare in Atlanta. I didn't need the sideways glances from those with me to tell me why that was.

I'm the reason this is centered in Atlanta.

I have no doubt in my mind if I decide to move cities or even countries, this clusterfuck will move with me. Bile rises in the back of my throat at the thought of how many humans have lost their lives. Collateral damage as Cass would call it.

Eric's hand brushes mine when he shifts next to me.

He is as anxious as I am, no matter how much he tries to hide it. I didn't know Satanael had a past with the Order, not that it would've changed anything. Maybe I would've been prepared to deal with things better now. Too little, too late.

"We should just go in and deal with it." Moving from foot to foot, I don't look away from the safe house. "It's not like they've seen Satanael before. How would they know who he is? They hate all of us equally." A nervous laugh passes my lips.

"I do not want to hurt them if it'll upset you," Satanael growls from my right. "I have done enough damage trusting others with your safety and wellbeing."

It should make me feel better, but it doesn't.

"I can go scare the shit out of them," Colt offers, standing on the other side of Satanael. "They hide when they see me coming."

"We all hide when we see you coming. That's because you're an asshole, not because we are afraid."

My words elicit a burst of surprised laughter from my father. I shrug a shoulder when he looks at me, hiding my smile. Beelzebub's deep belly laughter, however, stretches my lips wide. Shaking my head, I roll my shoulders to relieve the tension. We have to get inside the wards, but I really don't want my fellow hunters to leave the safe house so they get killed, or worse, for them to fight my father inside it.

"Oh, screw this!" Riling myself up, I take the first step. "Let's just go and deal with whatever happens."

My most famous words just before everything turns to shit, I know.

The wards prickle my skin as I walk through them, Eric not leaving my side. Stopping just inside, I turn to watch Beelzebub come through first, followed by Colt. Satanael keeps his gaze on mine when he takes a few measured steps, joining us on the other side. I see him shudder slightly, the feathers on his wings rustling. From one blink to the next, the burgundy wings are gone.

"You could've done that sooner. Maybe I would've stopped freaking out then." Waving a hand at his back, I frown at him. "I thought they had to be out for whatever reason."

"You could've asked me." One of his eyebrows, crusted with dried blood, lifts up.

"You were walking through hallways and bumping the shit out of them everywhere, so how was I supposed to know they could disappear?" I swear all of them are doing things on purpose just to piss me off.

"I was too weak to pull them in." Smiling slightly, he moves his shoulders around, no doubt, enjoying not having all that weight drag on them. "I'm almost back to normal now that I restored myself."

Beelzebub and Colt disappear through the front door, and Narsi decided to follow them, leaving the three of us in the front of the building alone. If I weren't tired and covered in gore, I would've enjoyed the daylight on my skin. It's not meant for me to enjoy anything lately, so I'm not surprised.

"Having the chains off helped, huh?" Stalling, I take a chance on some small talk. I should've known that nothing goes easy for me.

"The chains?" Satanael laughs. "That wore off the moment you took them off. I fed, so I'm back to normal."

Eric groans again. It looks like he resorted himself to just grunts and groans as a form of communication again. I, on the other hand, am ready to puke.

"You drank their blood?" Watching Satanael in horror, my stomach rolls. "Oh, my God…you ate them like Narsi!" Turning my anger on Eric, I jab a finger in his face. "You made fun of me for thinking all of you ate humans, but oh no! You wouldn't do that. You are cannibals, eating yourselves like that."

"What is she talking about?" My father looks taken aback. "I fed on their anger, child. What cannibalism?"

"Oh…" Feeling like an idiot, my face burns in embarrassment when Eric shakes his head wordlessly.

"Hel!" Cass pops her head out through the doors, a huge relieved smile blooming on her face. "You're back alive!" Squealing, she runs, throwing herself at me.

"Barely." Stumbling back a step, I hug my friend, a nervous laugh falling from my lips.

"Eww, you're nasty." Scrunching up her nose, her large brown eyes twinkle with humor. "First, you need to soak for an hour before you can go around people." Finally, she looks around us, smiling at Eric before her eyes land on Satanael.

"Oh, hi." Her gaze flicks from him to me.

Her lips form an O as I assume what is understanding hits her when she takes in the resemblance in our eyes. She swallows thickly, and my heart stops, expecting her to look at him with fear or hatred. But this is Cass, my friend that sees the good in everyone, including the Devil himself, it seems.

"You are Helena's father." She recovers quickly, smiling at him and reaching a hand at his chest. "I'm Cass, her teammate."

Satanael, remembering my declaration that I'm a hunter, stiffens for a second, and my hands clench into fists. I'm going to deck him if he says one word to upset her. He must've noticed because his shoulders relax, and he smiles back at her.

"I'm Satanael." Taking her hand, he gives it a pump before releasing her. "Pleasure to meet you Cass, Helena's teammate." He had to add that last jab, and the smirk on his face says it was on purpose.

I bristle, but Eric's hand on my back calms me down.

Cass, oblivious to the tension, smiles brighter and grabs my father under his arm like they are best friends now. The shocked look on his face is priceless.

"Let's get inside." Cass tugs him with her. "All of you need to wash that gore from your faces."

Eric and I follow behind them, bewildered by the whole interaction. "Well, that went easy." Eric breathes.

He jinxed us.

Chapter Nineteen

Taking my friend's advice, we usher my father through the hallways in a rush, almost jogging to one of the empty rooms Eric had set up for him. After giving him a change of clothes from Beelzebub, since only those will fit his massive frame, we left him with instructions to stay there until we come back to get him.

Hopefully, he'll listen.

Now Eric is leading me back to our room, his callused fingers so tight around mine you'd think he is preventing me from escaping. I have no intention of going anywhere, but I don't tell him that. If anything gets Eric passionate enough, that will be the uncertainty in my unstable emotions. It makes things more fun.

Hiding my smile, I lag one step behind him, watching his shoulders swing with each movement he makes. Butterflies are fluttering in my stomach, the anticipation building to a boiling point. I'm proud I don't jump on him here in the hallway. The last thing I need is Satanael seeing us naked. That thought makes me chuckle out loud.

Eric turns his head, looking at me over his shoulder with hunger in his gaze and one eyebrow lifted in question. I smile brighter, but don't say a word. It only pushes him to walk faster, dragging me along with him. Another giggle comes from me, making him groan. Heat pools between my thighs at the sound. We tease each other enough to self-combust at any moment, and I can't wait until we reach the damn room.

When my arousal perfumes the air, Eric turns around, nostrils flaring. Flipping me over his shoulder in a fireman grip, he jogs down the hallway. His fingers pressing into my thighs so I don't fall off dig into my skin through the pants, and I moan, unable to stop myself. As if that was an invitation, his hand glides up, those same fingers pressing at my core and rubbing gently. Eyes rolling into the back of my head, I squirm on his shoulder, my hands gripping the round globes of his ass.

"Hurry, Eric."

My hair swings wildly around his thick thighs when he starts full on running, almost plowing someone when we round a corner. He doesn't apologize, of course, and I'm too far gone to even care. Drowning in lust, his fingers still moving between my thighs, I giggle incoherently, hoping we are close to our room. Finally, he stops, opening a door and slamming it shut with his leg. My feet touch the floor the next second, but I have no time to react when both his hands twist my top, shredding it to ribbons. All I manage is a gasp before my bra suffers the same faith.

"You pushed me too far this time, Hel." The snarl was supposed to be an apology, I guess, but it raises goosebumps on my skin as I watch his face twist with barely contained lust.

Good, because I'm too far gone as well, and I want him wild.

Gripping my shoulders, he turns me around, one of his hands extending his claws that he uses to tear my pants at the seams. The room spins when I'm moved in a circle, my arms shooting out reaching for a grip, and my palms hit the wall just in time to prevent breaking my cheekbone in the process. Laughing, I look over my shoulder to see him ripping his own pants off, his erection bobbing out and slapping his belly. My core clenches air at the sight, while wetness coats my thighs.

"Eric…" His name is a moan, and I press my hips firmer into his hand.

Without a word, and with his gaze locked between my legs, he grabs my hips, lifting me up slightly before burying himself to the hilt. I'm wet enough to take all of him, but his girth still sends a burning sensation that only amplifies my pleasure. Even mindless with lust, he stops to look at my face, making sure I'm okay.

"Fuck me, don't just stand there." Pushing the words through clenched teeth, I jerk my hips towards his groin, moaning when he sinks in deeper. "Now, Eric. Move!"

That breaks whatever tiny thread of control he is holding onto. My fingers helplessly scrape at the wall to keep me from sliding down. Eric pistons at my back, his cock sliding in and out so fast I'm sure I'll be deliciously sore, and the back of my thighs will be bruised from the force of his pumps. With each thrust, the blunt head of his erection hits my womb, the pleasure and pain mixing together and making me delirious from it. We waited too long for this, partly because of my stubbornness, and partly from others being around us, and because of that, I'm almost ready to burst, but I fight it with everything in me. I don't want this to end too fast. I missed having him inside me.

My feet are lifted off the floor, giving Eric a new, deeper angle, and the second time he slams inside me, bright colors burst behind my closed eyelids, my mouth opening in a soundless scream as I convulse in his hands. He doesn't stop, his cock pumping harder in and out of me, prolonging my orgasm to the point that I get dizzy, and I'm afraid I'm going to faint. Luckily, I hold onto consciousness, and tremors shake my frame when he pulls out, lifting my limp body in his arms. I hear my voice from a distance, some incoherent words passing my lips as I watch his stern face through half-lidded eyes. The smile he gives me melts my heart before my back sinks into the mattress.

"I'm nowhere near done with you, Hel."

Crawling over me, his mouth slams on mine, his tongue pushing past my lips in a hungry kiss. Our tongues tangle together in a dance known since the beginning of time, our jaws opening so wide like we are ready to devour each other. Maybe we are. I know I can never get enough of him and, judging by the way he is crushing my body to his, neither can he. His sizeable warm hand takes my breast, massaging it tightly before he takes my hard, pointed nipple between his fingers. Pulling away from me, I watch him as his swollen, wet lips close around my sensitive, hardened peak, sucking it in before he lashes it with his tongue.

My fingers tangle in his hair, gripping it tightly so I can hold him there. His other hand pushes my legs apart, his thumb finding my button while two thick fingers enter me at the same time. My hips jerk up, gyrating in tune with the pumping of his hand. The rubber band in my belly starts tightening again, my still-sensitive flesh protesting and relishing his ministrations. My deep moans are loud, and I get crazier when I hear Eric's joining the sync. He is enjoying giving me pleasure as much as he is taking it, and I fall apart in his hands for the second time. My back bows off the bed, almost pushing him off me, but this time, I can't stop the scream shredding my vocal cords. He silences my shriek with his mouth, swallowing the noise I'm making, his chest vibrating with a feral growl. When I finally drop like a wet noodle on the bed, he lifts his head, grinning at me.

"My turn."

I just nod, or I think I nod, and he pushes my legs apart with his thick thighs. Through barely open eyes, I see his erection sticking out from between them, an angry red color accusing me of being selfish while he had to wait. Gathering as much strength as I can. I wrap my legs around his narrow hips, pulling him inside me. Eric sneaks a hand under my back, lifting my hips up in his lap, and then he starts moving. I don't know how it's possible since I'm only capable of breathing at the moment, but my body responds to him.

The sound of skin slapping skin fills the room, his testicles hitting my ass cheeks with each pump of his hips. After a second, my hips jerk on their own, meeting him halfway. My legs are shaking, and I can barely keep them around him, but I'm giving it my best effort when the tightening starts again.

"You are so tight I can barely move." Grunting, Eric keeps slamming inside me, proving his words false.

He feels fantastic, filling me up to the point of bursting as my channel clenches around him, sucking him in. I can see he is close to cumming, the lines on his face tightening with laser focus while he chases his own pleasure. I'm matching him breath for breath. His gaze, that is locked where we are joined, watches himself enter my body, then flicks to my face. My body stiffens as his eyes flash red, and I tighten around his cock so hard I'm not sure he can move for real this time.

Eric freezes above me a moment before he throws his head back, a deafening roar shaking the walls around us. My own scream disappears in the sound, and I feel warm jets bathing my insides as he jerks uncontrollably. When he finally drops on top of me, all I can do is wrap my arms around his shoulders before passing out with a goofy smile on my face. My last thought is, *I should piss him off more often.* And then I see only darkness.

Chapter Twenty

Eric

"You are pushing your luck, hunter." Satanael's voice is casual, but there is no mistaking the anger in it.

Glancing at Helena from the corner of my eye, I guide us through the door of the common area. My mate is tense, and she stiffens the moment her father's voice carries through the walls. My teeth are grinding in frustration. After I finally got her to myself, I made sure she forgot about everything else but her pleasure. I was crazed when we entered our room and took her so hard she couldn't even remember her own name.

A smile tugs at my lips.

Helena didn't mind at all. She gave as good as she took and then some. When she came around after the insanity of lust was slaked, I took my time. I made her scream my name over and over until I couldn't move a muscle even if jinn descended upon us. She was pliant in my hands, and a beautiful smile was etched on her face.

Now, this.

All I did to help her relax is for nothing the moment we leave our room. Satanael is not shy about expressing his anger. Maybe I was stupid to push her to free him. The fucker should've stayed chained until some sense got into his thick, stubborn head. Helena's hand tightens around mine when we see Satanael and the dumb hunter facing off in the middle of the common area. The human is either very brave or very stupid.

I'll go with stupid.

"I will not stay here while demons multiply daily like the plague." The hunter sneers. "I see no humans apart from us being protected, or angels for that matter."

I can see Satanael's hands clenching at his sides, impressing me with the control he is showing. I would've expected the hunters head to be rolling around by now. Maybe he really doesn't want to upset his daughter. Speaking of which…

"I can deal with this." Keeping my voice low, I tug on my mate's hand to get her attention.

"Because we need two arrogant men dealing with an

idiot, right?" She doesn't look away from the hunter as her gaze narrows and her lips press in a thin, white line.

Releasing my hand, Helena throws her shoulders back, striding straight between the two arguing males, leaving me with my mouth hanging open when I try to tell her that I was definitely not as arrogant as her father. Agitated for being dismissed, I'm about to call out so she looks at me, and the realization is like a bucket of cold water over my head.

"I am arrogant." Groaning at my own stupidity, I follow behind her.

"And how many angels do you personally know, asshole?" Squaring off with the hunter, Helena turns her back on Satanael.

The male looks like he swallowed a hot potato with her blunt dismissal of him. Satanael, just like my own father, is not used to anyone turning their back on him as if he is not a threat. Choking so I don't laugh out loud, I cough, bumping a fist over my chest. Satanael has murder written all over his face when he glares at me.

I smirk.

"Archangel Michael…" The hunter puffs up his chest like a pigeon in a cockfight, but Helena slices a hand in the air, cutting him off.

"That was a jinn. I was there if you remember. Try again." She glares at him.

"What would you know, demon lover." The hunter

takes a step closer, getting in her face. "And to think you were the Order's favorite."

The rest of the hunters are huddled together, watching everything wide eyed. Helena's two friends are standing before them, staring them down and daring them to get involved. Beelzebub and Colt are leaning on one wall, looking bored until now. As soon as the hunter's shoulders hunch aggressively towards Helena, the air thickens so fast I'm not sure how any of the humans are able to breathe.

Satanael turns into a stone statue.

My brother and Beelzebub push off the wall, the boredom on their faces turning to laser focus centered on the hunter obliviously ignoring the danger he is in. I'm fighting my own urge to rip his head off and stuff it up to his ass. At least someone was smart enough to keep the damn Haltija out of here.

None of us get the pleasure of taking our anger out on the idiot.

Helena's smile chills the blood in my veins. "Go on then." Waving a hand at the door behind me, she tilts her chin, urging him on. "Leave, oh pure one. See how long you stay alive on your own. We wouldn't want to taint your holiness."

The hunter's face turns such a vibrant shade of red that I'm surprised it doesn't explode. I see the twitch of his shoulders a second before his meaty arm swings at her head. Everything happens in slow motion after that.

Helena ducks, her arm shooting up, giving the hunter a perfect uppercut. His head yanks back from the force of her punch, spittle flying from his mouth in an arch around his face. The hunter's feet lift off the floor when his body follows, and Helena's other hand slams into the center of his chest, folding him in half before he flies back, hitting the opposite wall hard enough to crack it. It all happens so fast that all the rest of us have time to do is to blink.

Satanael moves behind her, his red wings bursting from his back like a cloud of doom. Gasps and shouts are like a distant echo in my ears as I watch my mate pivot on the balls of her feet, sending a round kick right at her father's sternum. Satanael crashes in the wall behind him with a comical look on his face.

Colt is already gunning for the hunter, which earns him Helena's forearm in his throat, lifting him off the ground and slamming him on his back to choke and cough so he can breathe. Beelzebub is the only aware one because he is standing in front of me, gripping my shoulders to keep me in place. I realize I'm struggling against him, so I stop moving.

You can hear a pin drop.

"Anyone else want to speak their mind on how they feel about me?" Flattening out invisible wrinkles on her top, Helena smooths down her hair with the calmest expression I've ever seen on her face. "No?" She looks around at all of us. "I didn't think so."

I gape at my mate when she walks up to a chair,

pulling it out and sitting down as if nothing happened. Colt is still gasping and writhing on the floor, Satanael is shaking his head to clear it, and the hunter is out cold in a heap on the ground. Beelzebub chuckles under his breath, hiding the sound like a pro. I know he is laughing because he still has an iron grip on my body.

"I'm hungry." Looking sheepish, Helena glances at me, her cheeks turning a lovely shade of pink. "I burned a lot of energy."

My lips tug in a smirk. What she means is I made sure she burned a lot of energy. My pants tighten instantly, and she rolls her eyes at me, but the smile stays on her face.

"Go feed your mate." Releasing a deep belly laugh, Beelzebub moves away from me, slapping my shoulder. "I would be kissing her feet if I were you, Shadow. The girl knows how to make an entrance."

A surprised chuckle makes me shake my head. "That she does."

I watch Cass walk up to Helena, giving her a high five with a grin that's almost splitting her face in half. Both women start chatting heatedly as they turn away from the rest of us. My mate's eyes look troubled, although she keeps up with her friend's excited conversation, the shorter woman waving her hands around to match the rapid-fire words coming out of her mouth.

"It's killing her to see her people turning against her," Beelzebub murmurs next to me. "Fools!" He spits the word like a curse.

"I know, and yet I can't do anything about it. She will never allow anyone to harm them." Giving the male a side-eye glance, I sigh. "She'll protect them while they are stabbing knives in her back, never doubt that."

"It must be nice to have loyalty like that." The wistful sound in his words snaps my head in his direction. "Relax cub, she sees nothing but you." Shaking his head, he jerks his chin at my brother. "Even the same face as yours doesn't stand a chance."

"I thought we were talking about the hunters." I watch my brother lift himself up, rubbing his throat. "You have her loyalty as well, old friend. She did drag your ass from Hell to save your hide, after all."

"I'm not sure if it was because she wanted to save me, or because I carried your unconscious ass on my back." Chuckling, Beelzebub winks at Helena when she turns our way.

"Remind me to never jump to your mate's aid, brother." Colt's voice is raspy, and he coughs as he winces. "Damn, the she-devil packs a punch."

"You're lucky she didn't stab you." Both Beelzebub and I laugh at Colt's face.

"I don't know why she protects the vermin." Satanael joins us, eyeing his daughter warily.

"Those vermin were her family until not long ago." Glaring at him, I make sure he gets it through his thick head. "Nothing you or anyone else can say will change that. You'd do well to remember my words if you ever hope for her to accept you hanging around."

"She had a family. I was tricked." Satanael sneers, but I don't back down. We can't fix what's been done.

"I think your conversation is long overdue. All I can say is, let her speak her peace before you start waving your wings and claws at her. She is more stubborn than all of us put together. You'll get more with honey than you will with vinegar."

"Who named him the wise one?" Satanael frowns at my brother and Beelzebub.

Both their fingers snap in Helena's direction, making me laugh.

Chapter Twenty - One

Helena

O kay, so I'm stalling.

As much as the hunter that I still can't remember the name of pisses me off with his shitty attitude, I must say punching him made me feel slightly better. I shouldn't have done it. It would've been better if I simply deflected his blow and stopped him from fighting, but I really needed that.

Munching on a multigrain bagel that Eric brought me, I force the bite down my throat when it tries to come up. The conversation with Satanael is a dark cloud threatening to pour icy rain over my head. Dread is eating me inside more than I'm able to eat the bread in my hands. Eric reaches towards my face, pulling my hand away from my mouth. I didn't even notice my teeth were gnawing on my nail instead of the food.

"He's like a ticking bomb." Keeping my voice low, I cover my mouth with the food in case Satanael can lip read.

"So are you, Hel." Smiling to lessen the blow of his words, Eric tucks a strand of hair behind my ear. "We need to know what he knows. Then we need to prepare for a fight because I can feel it coming. The jinn have been quiet too long for my liking." His mouth twists in anger. "And that fucker Mammon has to show his mug at some point."

"I'm not sure I want to know everything." Murmuring under my breath, I sigh. "Ignorance is bliss, or so they say."

"And that's going to change anything how? Knowing will change you as a person?" Huffing under his breath, he shakes his head. "If it were that easy, many things would've been different. I know it in my gut that you need to have all the details to be better prepared for what's coming. Hear him out. You are not obligated to take anything to heart that you don't like."

"Words have power, Eric." My trembling fingers almost drop the last piece of bread I'm holding. "Hearing things spoken can screw you up. If you keep telling a healthy person that they are sick, they'll eventually die believing it to be true."

His chest expands with the deep breath he takes. With a sigh, he takes my hand in his, peeking at me through his thick lashes. "And if I keep telling you that you are the most compassionate, loyal, and loving soul I know, would you believe that too?" When my gaze drops to the table, I can almost feel his disappointment in me. "I didn't think so. Bad things are easier to swallow, huh."

"What?" My head jerks up so I can look at him.

"Fear," he says simply. "Fear is a great tool if wielded correctly. It breaks a world as much as a person." Lacing his fingers through mine, he places our joined hands on his thigh. "But I know you, Hel. You don't just tilt your neck, baring it to be ripped. What you don't see is how powerful you are."

"I have weird powers inside me, Eric. They can destroy us all. You saw it yourself." I try to tug my hand away, but he holds on tight.

"You can destroy us all. And you"—Staring intently in my eyes, he sends a shiver racing up my spine—"will never do that, Hel. Your heart won't let you. I won't let you."

"You'll stand against me?" Making sure I understand him correctly, I search his gaze. Pain flashes through his dark green eyes.

"To save you from yourself?" Cocking his head, his lips press firmly together. "I will."

The rest of the chatter fades in the background as I stare at Eric. He has hidden things from me in the past, thinking I will not accept him for what he is. It hurt, but I can see why he hid it. Or twisted it in a way that he didn't have to tell me everything. But he never lied to me. Not when it really mattered, at least. It's not like I'm miss perfect, and I spill all my secrets to him, either. We all have our own demons that we keep close to our chest. I'm just one of those that have a demon in her bed, too. A demon that will give his life and his soul to do right by me, his handsome face open and vulnerable as he watches me with love and pride.

I believe him.

The fear lessens, loosening up my shoulders that feel like they were up to my ears with tension. With every new thing rearing its head up when it comes to whatever powers I have, the more weight there is pressing on me, drowning me in my own self-doubt. I have a good mask showing everyone I can carry them on my back without breaking a sweat, but deep down, I'm scared out of my mind that I'm not strong enough for that responsibility. I don't deserve the right to hold their lives in my hands.

I'm scared that I will break.

"The more time that passes, the more new powers are manifesting." Eric forges on, seeing me falter. "We need to know what we're up against when it comes to that so we can deal. You know it's the truth, Hel."

"At least we got Satanael out of the jinn's hands. It bought us time until they recoup for whatever they are planning." Blowing out a breath through pursed lips, I turn to look at my father. "I really thought you and your twin were the most arrogant jerks until I met him." Chuckling, I shake my head, making Eric smile. "The guy is a piece of work to be sure."

"He is bullheaded, yes. With every right, trust me." Leaning over, Eric presses a kiss on the side of my head. "He reminds me a lot of someone else I know."

"Not helping." Grumbling under my breath, I can't find heat to put in my words. "I wish Raphael was here."

The front door crashes open, echoing through the hallways. Everyone jumps to their feet, Eric yanking me behind him a moment before three large bodies fill up the threshold of the common room. Two dark haired men are carrying a limp, bloodied body between them, one I will recognize anywhere. My heart skips a beat when I lean over Eric's shoulder to see who broke into our safe house.

"Angels!" Satanael snarls his wings, popping out like a spring from his back.

"Helena?" The angel on the right locks his brilliant blue gaze on mine.

"Raphael!" As if my words have summoned him, the Archangel showed up at our door. Shoving Eric away, I run to them, dropping on my knees in front of the barely-awake man. "Raphael?" Lifting his head in my hands, tears leak down my face at the mess of blood and bruises. "What happened to him?"

"Michael," is all the two other angels say in unison.

Chapter Twenty - Two

"What the hell do you mean, Michael." Snapping at them, I cradle Raphael's head that is hanging limply on his shoulders, waving at Eric to come to help me. "He is missing, you idiots. It must've been a jinn."

"We know that now." The one on the left says, guilt written all over his beautiful face. He looks more like a girl if you ignore the muscled body that holds his pretty head on his shoulders. "Gabriel realized it too late. He almost lost his life, as well. Raphael refused to stay in Heaven, so we agreed to bring him here. The fool would've died if he left on his own."

Eric takes Raphael from the angels, lifting him in his

arms. He looks at me expectantly, and I shoulder my way past the two at the door, leading him to the first room I find. The bed is made like no one has slept in it, but there is clothing thrown around as if a tornado has gone past. Pointing at the bed with a shaking finger, I barely manage to stand still until Eric places the Archangel on it. Crawling on my knees, I loom over Raphael, unsure of what to do.

His hair is sticking out in all directions, and one of his eyes is swollen shut while his lips are split in a few places. His skin is more blue and purple than any other color. Both my hands hover over it, afraid to touch him in case I cause him more pain. I can feel bodies filling the room as everyone follows behind us.

"Why haven't you healed him?" Looking over my shoulder, I pin the two angels with a stern gaze. "Were you hoping he would die before bringing him here?"

"It wouldn't have been a great loss." Satanael sniffs, crossing his arms over his chest.

The ground shakes violently, sending everyone toppling around like pinballs.

"If you can't keep your mouth shut and you are not useful, get the fuck out!" Flinging my hand at the door where people are crowding to see what's going on inside, I glare at Satanael.

My father scowls at me but clams his mouth shut, thankfully. The two angels look ready to bolt out of here, their heads flinging left and right from me to Satanael and back. My heart is jackhammering wildly in my chest, every heartbeat more painful than the next, and red is clouding my vision. I can feel that fire building inside me and panic squeezes my throat. The last thing I want is to burn everyone here to ashes.

"Get out of my way." Cass's voice brings me back from the haze. I see people being shoved away at the doorway, the curls on her head bouncing when she pops out from between them. "Move, you idiots."

Holding a large bowl of water and rags fisted in one hand, she rushes to my side, ignoring the men staring at her like she's crazy. The water sloshes around when she moves past Eric and climbs on the bed on the other side of Raphael. Placing the bowl between her thighs, she shoves the rags in it, squeezing them out before handing one to me.

"We can clean him up while they get their heads out of their assess." She waves the wet rag in my face.

"Right." I'm not sure she is aware that she may have just saved everyone, so I hold onto her fingers for a moment longer than necessary to show my gratitude. Her firm nod tells me she knows exactly what she just did. "Thank you."

Both of us pretend we didn't hear the break in my voice. With gentle fingers, Cass moves Raphael's hair from his face, and we get to work, wiping away the blood wherever we can see it. Eric stands like a sentinel with his arms folded across his chest, growling at anyone that moves to approach the bed. I blink away the tears that threaten to fall out, pushing away the anger and fear for the Archangel's life. At least I can feel the faint beat of his heart when I clean up his chest. He is alive.

"Can someone please heal him now before I lose my shit?" When there is nothing more to clean up, I look up at my mate while addressing everyone in the room. "I'm holding onto control by a hair. I'm not sure how much longer I'll keep it up. I need him to speak, please."

"He didn't want us to heal him," one of the angels grumbles, leaning on the wall. "We tried, but he almost took my head off."

"Well, try it now," Eric snaps at him, and I want to kiss him.

"You better hold him down, Shadow, if you want me to try," the angel spits at Eric, and my mate lifts an eyebrow. "I know who you are."

"Good for fucking you!" Pushing the words through clenched teeth, I squeeze the rag in my hand, imagining the angel's neck right now. "First heal. Then talk."

Colt snorts from somewhere, and I know it is him because I'll recognize him with my eyes closed, but then he grunts, no doubt getting a punch from Beelzebub. I keep my eyes on the angel that is watching me like he's never seen a woman in his life. After a while, when I'm about ready to scream, he nods once, striding closer and reaching one of his large hands over Raphael.

Bright light pours from his palm, blanketing the

Archangel's chest. I release the breath I am holding. A soft breeze ruffles the hairs around my face, and the scent of flowers and sunlight saturates the air, filling my lungs. Without my control, my lips lift in a smile, the warmth from the angel's powers spreading through me like a blanket bathing me in light. Lifting my eyes from the angel's hand, I look at Eric. The strained lines around his mouth and eyes from the stress we've been dealing with are softened, and he gives me a reassuring nod. A horrible scream makes me jump a foot off the bed, and Cass does the same, sending the bowl of water flying at the angel.

Raphael roars again, his back bowing off the mattress so much it almost snaps him in half. The angel stumbles back, mouth gaping open and eyes as wide as dinner plates as he stares at the Archangel that is screaming like he is possessed. Not knowing what else to do, and in fear that he might die, I throw myself at him, my body curving on top of his bent chest. Wrapping both hands around him, I hold onto Raphael as if by sheer will alone I can keep him alive.

The building starts shaking hard, windows breaking in loud bursts of sprinkling shards around us. I realize I'm screaming as loud as the Archangel that is as tight at a coiled-up spring in my arms. Eric roars too, jumping on my back, to pull me off or protect me I don't know. His shadows dance to life, wrapping around the three of us like rubber bands holding us together. The moment they connect us, Raphael slumps down, soaking them up like a sponge, and we all drop on the bed, bouncing like a fish out of water. The silence is deafening in the room.

"Helena?" Raphael rasps, and my head jerks up so I can look at him.

"You are alive." It hurts when I speak, my throat raw from the screams.

"I am alive." Raphael smiles before his eyes roll to the back of his head.

Darkness takes me, as well.

Chapter Twenty-Three

Murmured voices penetrate the fog in my head. Like a distant buzzing of bees, they are annoying and insistent until they pull me awake. Pushing my face deeper into the pillow, I groan, unwilling to open my eyes. I feel like I've been hit by a truck, and I can sleep for a year before dealing with reality. Unfortunately, I'm not that lucky. Neither to sleep nor to even get hit by a truck. No, I have angels and demons to deal with instead.

"Gabriel needs to know about this." Raphael's voice jerks me up, and I fling my hair out of my face, twisting around to see him.

"Hel," Eric says my name loud enough to alert everyone that I'm awake. "How do you feel?"

"Not as good as Raphael, that's for sure," Satanael grumbles but offers a shrug, and a thin smile when I frown at him.

Looking around, I see we are still in the same room, only Raphael is standing next to the bed looking down at me while I'm stretched out on it. Guilt is like a hot poker in my chest, and I scramble off it in a rush. I surprise even myself when I throw myself at Raphael hugging him within an inch of his life. He doesn't push me away thankfully, choosing to instead wrap me up in his embrace while his shoulders shake with laughter. It's music to my ears to see him animated.

"Why are you standing up? You need to lay down so you can heal properly." Pulling away, I tug on his arm, pushing him towards the bed.

"I'm sorry I scared you, Helena." Taking both my hands in his, Raphael stops my frantic fidgeting. "I am healed, look at me."

He is right, of course, but that doesn't make me feel better. I can still smell the scent of blood in the air inside the room, making my stomach clench from the coppery stench. Feeling silly, I pull my hands out of his warm palms and plop down on the side of the mattress.

"What does Gabriel need to know?" Remembering what made me open my eyes, I change the subject.

The two angels are still here, looking wide eyed at all

of us from where they are leaning their backs on the wall, their faces whiter than the plaster behind them. Colt is stretched out on a cot someone shoved in one corner of the room, his hands folded under his head. He winks at me when I look at him, and I stick my tongue out, making him laugh. Beelzebub chuckles, shaking his head where he sits on the floor next to my father, both of them with their legs stretched out in front of them and crossed at their ankles. Eric rounds the bed, sitting next to me. He must've been standing over me while I slept. It sure sounds like something he would do.

"Why don't you tell me about your life, Helena," Satanael says softly, looking at me with dread as if I'm about to give him a ticket to death row. "I would like to hear it before I tell you everything."

"Why? So you know how to lie better?" He flinches at my snapped words, and I deflate like a balloon. "Sorry, that was totally uncalled for."

"I deserve it." Giving me a sad smile, he can't stop being himself when he adds, "Somewhat."

Raphael sits on the other side of me, placing me between himself and Eric. It shouldn't be something significant because we are all just sitting wherever, I know, but...it feels important to me. It gives me the courage to look back at my life and not cringe away from it. Or be ashamed of anything. So, with a deep breath, an Archangel on my left, and the prince of Hell on my right, I look the Devil in the eye, telling him my story.

Starting from the earliest years I can remember, I tell my father about Hector. How he cared for me and raised me the best he knew how. That I grew up knowing I was an angel blessed tasked with the responsibility of protecting humanity from the demons. They all chuckle and smile along with me when I tell them about my friends I grew up with, who later became part of my team. The moment my GPS started perking up, alerting me of evil being near, which I found out was a sense of self-preservation going off mostly when my life was in danger, or when a kindred soul was around me. Satanael nods at that as if it's normal, but I don't stop to ask him more about it. I still haven't fully figured that one out.

The air gets charged with anxiety when I get to the part when I met Eric for the first time. I can't stop the tears rolling down my cheeks when I tell him about Amanda, how hard it was on me when I lost my best friend. My father nods at Raphael in thanks when he hears about me being taken and the Archangel helping Eric to free me. I can see he has a lot to say about that, but he stays quiet, listening to the very end. He laughs heartedly when I tell him about my trip to Hell and the encounter with Lucifer before he was taken as well. Satanael looks troubled when I offhandedly mention that the clocks in Lucifer's castle started ticking, so I rush to finish my story before I bombard him with questions.

"They tried to take Raphael next." Rounding it up, I'm grateful for Raphael and Eric's silent support. "Luckily, we figured it out and stopped them from taking him. Something in me says three is a significant number to the jinn. They had you, Lucifer, and Mammon. Michael was missing, as well as my mother. I knew Raphael was the missing part in whatever they were planning, so we got to him on time. They haven't shown up after that."

I feel drained, barely able to keep my eyes open after talking for so long. My head drops on Eric's shoulder, and I smile when Raphael takes my hand in his, squeezing my fingers gently. Satanael watches the three of us with a thoughtful expression, and even Beelzebub slightly narrows his gaze, seeing something that I'm totally missing.

"So, no one told you who your parents were until Shadow found you?" My father flicks his gaze from me to Eric.

We both shake our heads at the same time.

"The jinn pretending to be Michael said I'm half angel half demon the night he tried to kill me…when Amanda died." Blinking back the tears that try to flood my eyes again, I sigh. "He didn't give names. They all left that for Lucifer. He was kind enough to enlighten me on my family tree."

"Very well." Satanael nods once. "I think it's time you hear the truth."

Chapter Twenty - Four

The seriousness of Satanael's face twists me into knots, and I'm grateful for Eric's and Raphael's calm presence. Even Colt straightens up, giving levity to the situation that I didn't need. I can already tell that that I'm not going to like whatever comes out of my father's mouth.

"Many tried before to create a child made out of Heaven and Hell." His eyes glaze over, Satanael losing himself in his memories. "No matter where they kept the offspring, one or the other side ended up killing them long before they reached maturity."

"When Zadkiel came to me with her offer, I dismissed her on principle alone. I had no time to get involved with their schemes, no matter how right they were. We had all lost our way by then. Darkness and light, alike. A child wasn't going to fix it, or so I thought."

Raphael stiffens next to me when my father's gaze focuses on him. I tighten my hold on his hand, hoping it'll soften whatever words we are about to hear.

"Raphael was happy to hear me denying your mother. Everyone knew his love for her had no bounds. Isn't that right, old friend?" There is no malice in the comment, so I keep my mouth shut, even when the Archangel stays coiled up next to me. "But, so much like you, Zadkiel was nothing if not determined. Especially when angels and demons started disappearing with no trace. All of us started looking over our shoulders, getting paranoid about who will be next. None of us suspected the jinn. They were supposed to be the balance. The laws that kept us from destroying ourselves and the worlds with our never-ending wars. So, I caved, much to Raphael's displeasure, after Lucifer agreed he will have his first born protecting the child."

Satanael turns to me next, and numbness covers my body like a blanket. I'm barely breathing, my chest feeling tight from his intent gaze. It's Eric's turn to jerk upright at hearing those words. My father continues, ignoring our reactions.

"When you were born, your mother convinced me that she would hide you where no demon or angel would be able to set eyes on you. I trusted her with your life. I never wanted a child, but that didn't mean I didn't want you when you were born. You were mine, and you'll always be mine."

A lump forms in my throat when his eyes shimmer for a moment with unshed tears. Is it an act, or does he really care that much? I have no time to wonder because his confession continues.

"I never thought Zadkiel would be crazy enough to place you in the Order. The pain in the ass organization that we couldn't get rid of, and Heaven stayed away from, washing their hands of them a long time ago."

"She didn't place Helena there," Raphael speaks with a head bowed, his voice thick with emotion. He wouldn't look at me, either. "I did. I convinced Michael that she would be trained, and we could use her in the war as a weapon against Hell. I did it for Zadkiel."

A tear trickles down my face at the pain I see in Raphael's eyes when he finally lifts his head. How much has it hurt him to watch the woman he loved have a child with someone else, and then take responsibility for protecting it, too?

"The last eighteen or so years have been one fight after another, all of us at each other's throats for no reason at all. Even those of us that were friends and allies." Satanael looks away from my tear-streaked face. "I decided to find out who was turning our lives into a nightmare and went looking for your mother. When I found her, she told me that I was just in time because your life was in danger. Without question, I followed her to the human realm, only to find out that it wasn't Zadkiel that met me. It was a jinn disguised as your mother that lured me there where I'm at my weakest, and they trapped me in that damn brick contraption they called their base of operations. I was kept there until the lot of you found me, plotting how I will make them pay for what they've done."

A shiver makes me tremble when his power sends a pulse through the air around us.

"That still doesn't explain anything." My voice breaks, and I have to clear my throat to be able to speak. "There is no way the jinn destroyed everything, murdered so many, just to kill a hybrid like myself."

"But you are not just any hybrid, now are you?" Satanael searches my face for something, and a line forms between his eyebrows when he doesn't find it. "You are the mercy and love of Heaven and the wrath and cunning of Hell. Light and shadow blended together and turned into the ultimate weapon. A ruler in your own right. Creator of your own laws and punisher to all of us if you feel so inclined." His eyes lock on the blade still holstered on my thigh. "The idiots gave you a blade etched with sigils to summon mine or Zadkiel's powers at your whim, in their arrogance thinking they are invincible. I guess you showed them the error of their ways." Chuckling, Satanael shakes his head.

I don't find any of it funny.

"Still, I don't understand what you're telling me. Can you stop with the fucking theatrics and just spit it out already?" Grinding my teeth, I glare at him, because if not then I'll start crying. "What the fuck am I?"

"You took the power from the jinn, Helena. You are *the* balance in the creation of life. While the rest of us, angel or demon, weaken when we enter the human realm, you are the strongest here. This is your realm. *You* rule this realm like Lucifer does Hell, and Michael does Heaven. You, my child, can let us live or die at your liking, and there is not a thing any of us can do about it." Beaming at me with pride, Satanael laughs at my slack jaw. "And I am your father!"

My wild gaze searches the room for anyone to deny his claims. I'll take being called an evil abomination or a demon lover at this point, too. The two angels look even paler, staring at me with reverence and fear. They both look like they are about to puke. And so am I, for that matter. Jumping off the bed, I only manage two steps before emptying my stomach all over two large, black boots.

Chapter Twenty-Five

"I think she did this on purpose," Colt grumbles, grimacing at his puke-covered boots as he lifts one foot off the floor. "I always end up with the short end of the stick."

"That's because you are a jerk, not for anything else." Accepting the glass of water Raphael fetched me, I have to use both of my hands, or I'll spill the water all over myself.

All of us look like we are about to keel over. Different shades of white and green are the tones of our skin while Satanael looks positively radiant, the stupid smile still plastered on his face.

"I don't want it." When no one reacts to my words, I

clear my throat, speaking louder. "I said, 'I don't want it.'" My chin lifts stubbornly when I look down my nose at my father.

"You don't want what exactly?" The smile slips from his face, and I want to high five myself.

"Any of it." Waving a shaking hand, I grapple for the glass when it almost slips from my hold. "All of it. You name it, I. Don't. Want. It!"

"That's not how this works." Lifting himself up, he looks down at me from his height. He is a head taller than Eric, so I have to crane my neck to stare him in the eye. "It's what you are. You don't get to choose if you want it, just like the rest of us."

"Watch me!" I snarl in his face, and he jerks back with a stunned look on his face.

Eric groans.

"Eric, if you keep on groaning, first, I'm going to stab him." I point a shaking finger at my father before turning it on him. "Then I'm going to cut you."

"At least I'm out of this one," Colt mumbles and my head snaps his way.

"You will be third!"

"What in the worlds did I do now?" Watching me incredulously, both his palms lift in a placating gesture.

"You're breathing." Glaring at him, I bare my teeth in a mockery of a smile. "It pisses me off."

"I think we should leave," one angel says to the other, shifting restlessly on his feet while he eyes me warily.

"No one is going anywhere until we agree that I have nothing to do with any of you. Or anything else." Nodding as if that will fix everything, I walk up to Eric and plop next to him again.

It speaks volumes how shocked he must be since he hasn't moved from his perch on the mattress. Not even when I was sick all over his brother's boots. Why Colt was standing there instead of being stretched out on the cot, I have no idea, nor do I care. He should know better than to move unpredictably around me.

I don't want to move unpredictably around me.

"I can do that, right?" Speaking under my breath, leaning into Eric, I wrap my cold fingers around his upper arm. "Like I'm quitting a job. I'm done, and they can do whatever they want."

"I'm pretty sure this doesn't work like that, Hel." Prying my stiff fingers off his arm, he tucks me under it, kissing the top of my head. "It'll be fine. We'll figure it out."

"I don't want to figure it out, Eric." I meant to whisper, but my shout turns every head in the room in my direction. "I want all of them to leave me alone. I'm not doing anything, and you can't make me." Glaring at my father, I make sure he knows I'm talking to him in particular.

I'm acting like a child, I know, but I'm freaked out, and my body is trembling because I'm so cold I'm freezing, while dark spots dance at the corners of my eyes. Even my chest hurts because I can't seem to get enough oxygen in my lungs that are slowly shriveling inside me.

"I did make you, and this is not a job you can quit." Confirming that even when I was whispering he was eavesdropping, Satanael doesn't back down.

"Back off, Satanael. She needs time to process all this." Eric snarls, finally shaking off his shock.

"I would watch my tongue if I were you, Shadow, before you piss me off."

"I will watch nothing when you are glaring at my mate!"

The building does a violent lurch, followed by shouts from behind the closed door. Squeezing my eyes shut, I push the fear and anger down, struggling to keep control of it. My heart does a hard thump against my ribs, and another wave of power bursts from my chest, shuddering the safe house. Crashing noises echo through the hallway, many running footsteps passing our room.

"Shit, she's gonna blow!" Colt's shout gets everyone in motion.

Eric snatches me in his arms, bolting out the open door that Beelzebub holds for him. We topple a few people over when we barrel through the hallways, my body stiff as a board while I'm grinding my teeth. The only thing helping to keep control over my power is the fear that I might hurt Eric. He is too close for me to go all nuclear here. Exploding in Hell is one thing. Doing it in the middle of Atlanta while the man I love holds me in his arms is a totally different story.

"Just breathe, Helena." Raphael's worried face pops up over Eric's shoulder. "Deep breaths. You can control it. I know you can."

"I'm not sure I can."

Satanael is yelling Eric's name, but we all ignore him as we turn through the never-ending hallways until I can see the front doors of the safe house.

"The wards will protect everyone from the blast?" Eric sounds panicked, and it only makes things worse for me. I forgot he saw me go kaboom in front of his father's home.

And he is still alive. Just let go. The inner voice purrs in my head, scaring the shit out of me.

"I'm not sure." Raphael is right on our heels.

We burst through the doors, Eric jumping all the stairs in one go, his boots thumping heavily on the ground from our combined weight. I can't turn my head, and every muscle in my body is as stiff as a rock, but I see the rest of them following behind us like they have a death wish. I know the last time this happened, Eric was about to die, and there were hordes of demons at Lucifer's gates. My anger was aimed at them, so no one else but our enemy got hurt.

There is no enemy right now to take the force of the storm brewing inside me.

I'm not even angry, just shitless scared.

My body starts shaking violently in Eric's arms. The cold I was feeling earlier spreads to the marrow of my bones and my teeth are chattering from it. Not even the string for curses coming from Eric can lighten up my mood. If I don't kill them all, I'll kill myself. It feels like my skin is slowly ripping apart, unable to contain the force of nature inside me.

We exit the wards, and Eric stops, turning left and right, not knowing where to take me. I didn't even feel that we passed the wards on my ice-frosted skin.

"She's in shock." Raphael's voice is distant, coming from so far away, yet I see his face right in front of my eyes.

"Put me down, and rrr...rrun." Stammering, I almost bite my tongue off, pushing weakly on Eric's shoulders. "Gggoo…"

"Like fuck I'm leaving you alone!" Snapping at me, he tightens his hold.

Stupid man.

A scream is ripped from my throat when a strong pulse of power flings me out of Eric's hold, dropping me on my hands and knees. Panting like a crazed person, I lift my face, looking around me through strands of my hair. All of them are spread around in a semicircle, watching me like fate has made them my judges. Through blurry eyes, I see my father step closer, his hand reaching for me, getting larger and more extensive the closer it gets. The moment he touches my shoulder, I slump down, half of the pressure lessening, yet I still feel like I'm about to explode.

"Little help here."

He snarls at someone a moment before I see Raphael approach me, his hand stretched out, reaching for me. My arms are shaking, barely able to hold my weight as short puffs of air lift the hair off my face. When the Archangel's fingers curl around my other shoulder, the force inside me disappears in a whoosh. Their combined grip on my shoulders is the only thing that stops me from faceplanting on the street.

Chapter Twenty-Six

"What the hell was that?" I cling to Eric where he sits on the sidewalk, holding me between his thighs and cradling my head on his chest.

"I think I know why the jinn are trying to get three Archangels and three fallen for their goal." Beelzebub looks ashen, his troubled eyes locked on my face.

After Satanael and Raphael stopped me from exploding and killing everything in sight, I was hugging both of them at the same time, making them fidget uncomfortably. I didn't care. It wasn't like it was done in gratitude. It was for selfish reasons. I was scared that if I stopped touching them, I'd feel that horrible pain and cold again. Eric had to yank hard on my arms, so I released my hold.

I'm not even embarrassed about it.

Eric takes a breath, and I dig my nails in his forearms, cutting off the question I know is coming, but I don't want to know the answer to. They can keep their information and knowledge to themselves. I've had enough of it. It doesn't stop Beelzebub from talking, unfortunately.

"What would you do, Helena, if you felt your power surging that strongly again?" the large fallen asks, and my gut clenches in remembrance of the pain. My eyes lock on Satanael and Raphael instantly, and Beelzebub nods, grunting. "I thought so."

"I used to like him." Forcing myself to look away, I turn to Eric. "Remind me how stupid that idea is next time I say that."

Eric just kisses my forehead, pressing my face firmer to his chest. Beelzebub chuckles softly, the sound grinding on my nerves right now.

"You still feel your power just under the surface ready to push up at any moment," he prods. Although I ignore him, I search inside me to see if he is right. My shoulders stiffen when I realize he is telling the truth, and that's enough of an answer for him. "If I had three Archangels and three fallen at my disposal, I'd be able to help you keep control of it, no questions asked. In return, so you don't feel the horrible pain, you'll do anything I ask just so you don't go insane and kill the entire human race. Or yourself."

I don't think I've ever hated anyone as much as I hate Beelzebub right now. Deep down, I know that he is not saying things to hurt me or because he gets off on seeing me suffer. He is trying to help, and understanding the situation is key for us to stop the jinn. Still, I can't help it when I hiss at him like Narsi has been rubbing off on me. If he keeps blabbing, I'm at a point where I might take a bite of his face, too.

"I'll kill myself before I let that happen."

"Okay, that's enough!" Colt glares at all of them, and I see my father's eye twitching. "Are you all brainless? She is twenty years old, not centuries like the rest of you idiots! You are used to dealing with facts and playing your games on how to stay on top. Can't you fucking see you are scaring the life out of her? Are you trying to help her or kill her?" His face is twisted in anger as he snarls at all of them. "I can't watch this shit show anymore!" Throwing his hands in the air, he storms away, heading through the front doors of the safe house.

"I must admit, I might've been wrong about Colt this whole time," I tell Eric, who is staring at his brother's back with his jaw hitting the top of my head.

"I agree." My mate sounds like he can't believe his own words.

"Helena, we are not trying to scare you. We are looking for ways to protect you." Beelzebub looks hurt.

"I know that." Taking a deep breath through my nose, I release it slowly. "And to think that I thought the worst thing that could happen to me is for the jinn to use me to open the gate of Hell with my blood." Giggling nervously, I wipe my sweaty palms on my pants.

"They don't need your blood to open a gate to Hell or to Heaven." Satanael frowns at me.

"Yes, they do." A tremor passes through me just thinking about it. "When the jinn that looked like Michael kept me a prisoner, he took a shit ton of blood. They use it to go from one realm to the other." My voice trails off because my father is already shaking his head.

"They don't need it to open gates." Satanael looks from me to everyone else and back. "They use your blood to hold onto any form they take. Without it, they can only disguise themselves for a short period of time."

The blood curdles in my veins, and I feel lightheaded. My father and Raphael scramble around, crowding me, their hands grabbing onto the first thing they can reach. The Archangel is holding my ankle in his hand, and my father is bruising my forearm. A hysterical laugh bubbles out of me.

"I helped them kill so many people." Swaying, although I'm sitting down, I blink fast to clear my vision. "They turned Heaven and Hell inside out, and I made that happen. My cursed blood made that happen."

"Stop that nonsense," Raphael snaps at me, and it instantly pulls me out of the misery that is pulling me under. "This is not like you, Helena. I think the shock and these new powers are making your emotions unstable. Maybe you should rest more. When you wake next, we will talk about how to proceed. I have watched over you for twenty years as I promised your mother," He nods at me sternly. "I have no intention of failing now when you have reached your prime."

"Neither do I," Eric grumbles at my back.

"I have known you for a little over twenty-four hours." Satanael smiles sheepishly. "But as I said before, you are mine, and you'll always be mine."

I find it funny to see the two angels nodding in agreement since they were quietly observing the whole fiasco, and I'm guessing doing their best to stop their eyes from popping out of their heads. I bet they don't have freak shows like this in Heaven. I should ask Raphael after I take his advice and go have a long nap. As if he called it, my eyelids feel heavy, dropping low over my eyes.

"Maybe a power nap." My jaw cracks when it stretches wide in a yawn.

"Just close your eyes." Eric kisses the top of my head, and I drift off with all three of them holding onto me like I'm about to escape.

I wish I could.

Chapter Twenty-Seven

Eric

"I need to know how to keep her safe." Keeping my voice low, I resort to begging Satanael because I'm scared I'm going to lose my mate. "And remember, she is not your subject or a toy for you to play with. If you want to stay in her life, start putting a leash on your attitude."

"He knows from experience." Raphael chuckles good-naturedly, and I nod to confirm his words.

"There is nothing wrong with my attitude." Satanael scowls at me, offended.

I don't say anything, just stare at him until he scoffs,

looking away. My advice was me offering peace to him before, if need be, I force information on how to keep Helena protected. With my father out of the picture, for now, Satanael is my best bet. Beelzebub doesn't get involved much in the politics of the realms, and Leviathan is the fates knows where, following Maddison. The Archangel and his angels are useless, not knowing much about the jinn since they never feared them, thinking they can't do wrong. The joke is on them. My mate's father is the only help I can get.

"How do I keep her safe?" I'll keep asking until he gives me the answer.

"What my brother is trying to say is: How do *we* keep her safe?" Colt pipes in, lifting an eyebrow when I can't stop my growl. "Easy killer. She's all yours. The she devil made it abundantly clear from day one. But let me tell you one thing." Leaning his forearms on his knees, my brother squints at me. "Any woman that can gut a demon like a fish has my respect. One like your mate, who is capable of disintegrating jinn, has me clenching my ass cheeks singing yes ma'am any day."

The two angels burst out laughing, surprising themselves as they choke on their tongues, trying to cover it up. Everyone else laughs, including Satanael, his chest puffing out in pride. He should be proud of a lot more than Helena's fighting skills, but I don't feel the need to remind him of that. I need him in a good mood, so I nod my thanks to my brother. Checking to make sure Helena is still sleeping, I look expectantly at Satanael.

"I take it Gabriel is not in a chatty mood?" He turns to Raphael instead of answering me.

"If he has recovered, he might be." Raphael rubs a hand over his face. "He was worse than me the last time I saw him. We honestly didn't see it coming."

"You knew Michael was missing, so what do you mean you didn't see it coming?" My fists are clenching at the stupidity of it.

"I know he is missing," the Archangel snaps before his shoulders slump. "We found him barely alive at the entrance of the portal. We believed it was our brother and that he somehow escaped. It was a pretty good trap. I was also worried about Helena, so I wasn't thinking straight."

"Just like me," Beelzebub grumbles. "I'm usually pretty good at judging her moods and choosing my words. I forgot myself earlier with all the tension."

"How about we all stop worrying about Helena?" Colt adds his two cents. "She doesn't need mother hens around her; she's very much capable of taking care of herself. What she needs is all of us using our brains. Unless none of you noticed, she will blow us to smithereens if she goes off. I kinda like my face, thank you very much."

"Leave it to you to get to the point with your vanity." The snark is missing in my words, and we both know it. My twin is surprisingly levelheaded lately. If his asshole side didn't poke its head once in a while, I'd think a jinn replaced him.

"How fast can we get Gabriel and one more of you here?" Satanael continues his interrogation of Raphael.

"I'd say a day." Glancing at the angels, Raphael nods thoughtfully. "Metatron was mulling around when I was there. If he is still around, I can have them both here in twenty-four hours, even if Gabriel is still hurt. We'll heal him here."

"Will Eric or me be enough to replace my father?"

"We won't need that." Satanael dismisses my brother with a flick of his wrist.

"No one knows when Leviathan will be back," I remind everyone unnecessarily.

"I don't need him." Satanael grins like a fiend. "Mammon will beg to help out after I get my hands on him tonight."

"Where the hell are you planning on finding Mammon? He is hiding like a rat sensing an earthquake coming." Maybe Helena was right. Satanael has lost his mind while chained on that wall.

"In the same place he had me pinned on the wall." When I frown at him, his grin grows. "He might want to hide, but he will show his face when he realizes I'm there to take my daughter's blood back. I'm pretty sure his friends won't take it kindly if he loses their only ticket in our midst."

"I like the way you think!" Colt claps his hands, rubbing them together. "When are we leaving?"

"No one said you are going." Satanael glares at him. "I'm going alone."

"This is why he was pinned to a wall." Beelzebub blows out a breath. "You can't just barge in there on your own. They'll nail your ass again. We do this together. All of us doing our own thing led us to this. No more running off alone."

"And I've been itching for a fight ever since I watched you slaughter all of them after you were freed. You have to share the glory, Satanael." Colt smirks. "For Helena, of course."

"Of course." If Satanael's voice were any dryer, dust would've been falling out of his mouth.

"This is a solid plan." Always calm, Raphael watches us warily. "We just forgot the most important thing."

"Helena will be fine with this. She wants the damn jinn out of the picture as much as the rest of us, if not more." Satanael waves it off.

"Who are we all going to swear loyalty to? Who will all of us trust to bind our powers to them for her sake? It can't be Helena, or this would not have been an issue." Raphael is barely breathing as he watches all of us. "I'm sure Gabriel and Metatron will want to know that first."

"Me." I feel like I'm about to hurl, but the words come easy from my lips.

"You are insane if you think I will willingly give you power over me." Satanael's face turns to granite.

Raphael is nodding his head, slowly keeping his gaze locked on mine. I can feel his power like prodding fingers, not in my head but at the center of my chest. Everything in me screams that I block him and rip his head off for even trying something like this on me. Pushing my instincts away for Helena's sake, I let him in. His eyes widen when he finds no resistance, but neither one of us says a word. Satanael must notice something is going on because he shuts his mouth, looking from me to the Archangel until an understanding rocks him on his feet. He stares at me slack jawed. I'm not sure that, to this point, he understands what I'm ready to do for my mate.

Like letting an Archangel look at my soul and every dark secret I've hidden there.

"You are ready to shoulder the consequences of that responsibility, as well, Shadow?" Raphael's words are hesitant and soft.

"What consequences?" Satanael demands arrogantly.

"Yes." My shoulders relax when the Archangel pulls back his power. "I will kill her if she can't handle her powers. I vow to protect you all if I can't save her." The words are bitter like poison on my tongue.

"Brother..." Colt's face is drained of blood as he drops on his knees. "You can't. It'll kill you."

"If I can't keep her alive, I'm already dead...brother." My jaw clenches when my twin's head bows in defeat.

Satanael stands still for a long time, watching me. After a while, he simply nods. Ignoring all of them, my gaze finds my mate curled up innocently on the bed. Just thinking that she won't be able to hold her control shreds my insides like I've swallowed shards. My heart is already bleeding, but I close it off, forcing myself to stay calm and collected for her sake. We will either both live a very long life, or we will both die in twenty-four hours.

I always said fate was a bitch.

Chapter Twenty-Eight

Helena

They are planning something.

Eric is clingy. Well, more clingy than usual. His eyes track every breath I take like he is reassuring himself that I'm alive. I know I scared him earlier when I almost self-combusted, but this still feels different. It's creepy as hell.

To make things worse, Colt looks like he is running for nun of the year, going out of his way to be kind to me. Maybe I woke up in a parallel dimension or something. Whatever it is, it makes the hairs on my neck stand at attention.

Adding to the ridiculous situation is the hunter I knocked out when we brought my father to the safe house. He looks like he swallowed a bug, gaping at Raphael and the angels with drool dripping from the corner of his mouth. I feel sorry for him, subtly wiping my own with the back of my hand, but he doesn't get the hint, and I give up. Now, I'm sitting at a table with a bowl of cornflakes, watching the stubborn men who made it their mission to annoy me talk quietly among themselves as they huddle in the corner of the room.

Eric is staring at me from there.

"Do you know what's going on?" Cass pulls out a chair to sit next to me, the scraping sound making me cringe.

"Nope." Ending the word with a pop, I shove a spoonful in my mouth. Chewing it quickly, I force it down my throat so I can speak. "And I'm so creeped out that I think I don't really care."

"I don't blame you." My friend stares at her own plate, letting the hair fall over her face to hide her mouth. "All of them were staring at you when I came to check on you in the room. Even the two angels. It scared the shit out of me. I thought you died in your sleep."

A burst of surprised laughter turns every head in our direction. Slapping a hand over my mouth, I find the cornflakes floating in the milk fascinating. When all of them look away, I lift my head, widening my eyes at Cass. She grins and shakes her head at my antics.

"I was really scared when I spoke to my father." Confessing my fears to my friend, I keep speaking low so that we are not overheard. "I think it was more the shock of it all that made me ready to go…" Not wanting to say the word, I make an exploding gesture with my fingers.

Cass nods in understanding.

"Raphael was right. I needed sleep and to process it all." Blowing out a breath, I smile when my friend wraps her fingers around mine. "Everything they told me changes nothing, just like Eric said. I keep searching for something different inside me, but there is nothing to find. I'm still me…just a little overwhelmed and maybe more than a little crazy."

"You were always a little crazy." Cass chuckles, squeezing my hand.

"Very true, only now I just added to it."

"You know I'll help any way I can, right?" Watching me through her lashes, her smile disappears. "I might not be as powerful as any of you, but I can kick demon ass with the best of them."

"If anyone knows that Cass, it's me. I want nothing else but for things to be the way they used to, but I don't want you hurt. It's selfish, I know," I hurry to explain myself when she opens her mouth. "I lost almost everyone I had as a family. I can't lose you or George. Please."

"And what about us?" A tear rolls down her cheek, breaking my heart. "Don't we get to say if we are willing to lose you? You are my family, too, you know."

"I'm not that easy to kill. You know this."

Wiping her tears, I stop talking when a shadow falls over us. When George sits on the other side of me, I know he has heard our conversation. He is not the type to just squat when girls are talking. One glance at his emotionless face confirms it. Blowing out a sigh, my cheeks puff out.

"All of them are immortal." Looking from Cass to George, I'm praying they'll understand my fears. "Apparently, so am I. We are impossible to kill. I will let the jinn kill me if your lives are in danger. Is that what you want?"

"That's not fair." Yanking her hand away from mine, Cass glares at me.

"It's not, but I need to know you are safe. At least for now. Please, Cass."

"What exactly are we talking about?" George squints at both of us, his deep voice rumbling in his chest. "Is there a fight I don't know about?"

"They are plotting, can't you see?" Cass flings a hand at the jerks huddled with their heads together, and Eric narrows his eyes at me. I yank her arm down.

"Stop pointing." Hissing, I glance at my mate, but he is not looking my way anymore, thankfully.

"Sorry." Folding her hands in her lap, she looks pointedly at George.

"So, what is our plan?" he asks Cass.

"Seriously, George?" It's been a while since I've wanted to slap him. "Do you want her to die?"

"No, of course not. But I don't want you to die either. So"—Looking from me to Cass, he grins—"what's our plan?"

"This is what I think." Cass leans in eagerly and starts talking a hundred miles an hour.

My mind shuts off when she gets to a point where if jinn ever come near the safe house, we will be using her as bait. The woman is insane, and so is George for playing along with her ludicrous ideas. They would've made a great production team if we lived near Hollywood.

Eric walking up to our table shuts them both up. He looks at all of us with suspicion, but after a moment, he loses interest in my friends. Reaching his hand towards me with his palm up, I place my fingers in his, letting him pull me to my feet. A shiver crawls up my spine like every time we touch skin to skin. His nostrils flare, and he tugs me closer to him.

"I know you slept, but a bit more rest might do you good," he murmurs in my ear, and I'm already clenching my thighs when I hear the hunger in his voice.

"Get a room, you two." Cass mockingly glares at us. "Some of us are pathetically single."

"I can fix that problem for you, sweetheart," Colt calls out, but his usual flirty manners are missing. Cass turns bright red, making me laugh. She does like the jerk.

I hear her grumble, "Whatever." Then, Eric leads me

out of the common room. As soon as we walk out the door, he stops, and I turn to look at him, confused what made him halt.

"I forgot to ask Satanael something. Go on, I'll catch up." He gives me a nudge, and I move away from the door until he disappears through it.

The moment he is gone, I hurry back, pushing the slightly open door just enough to peek through it with one eye. My teeth clench when I see Eric whispering something to Cass and George, and my friends nodding with determined faces. If he gets them in trouble, I'm going to find my guns and shoot his ass again while he sleeps. With one last nod, he turns away from them, and I bolt down the hallway to our room.

They can plot all they want, but so can I.

Chapter Twenty - Nine

My plotting died a sudden death the moment Eric stood naked in front of me.

A smile pulls my lips up, remembering all the things he did to me for hours. Stretching my arms over my head, I twist under the sheets, hoping I'll relieve the soreness for a bit. My mate knows how to scramble my brain so I can't even remember my name. I should keep him locked in this room for a few days. I'm sure he won't mind.

My eyes snap open when my hand finds his side of the bed empty and cold. Lifting my head up, I look around to see if he is in the room, and a scream splits the air when I see Cass looming over my head like some psycho.

"What the hell is wrong with you!" Shouting from the

top of my lungs, I clutch the sheet to my chest to keep my naked body hidden. "You have gone crazy, haven't you?"

"Finally, you are up." Clapping her hands, she grins at me. "I thought I would need to drag your bubble ass out of bed by your feet."

"You are nuts." She's lucky that crazy fire inside me stayed quiet and didn't blast her to kingdom come. "Where is Eric, and what are you doing here."

"I thought you'd never ask." Plopping on the bed with a flourish, she bats her eyelashes at me. "Your man left with the rest of the hotness on a mission that you apparently, just like the pathetic human here"—She points the finger at her chest look at me pointedly—"are not allowed to go on."

Confused, I just stare at her.

"I, on the other hand, was ordered. Not asked, mind you, but ordered by your hunk to do everything I can to keep you in this house. Well, not just me. George, too, but he was too scared of Eric to come inside the room while you are naked. Our life depends on you staying inside these wards." Saying all this in one breath, Cass sucks in a lungful of oxygen before bellowing loud enough to make my ears pop. "Get in here, George! She's awake!"

The door clicks open, and George pops his head in faster than I can process what is going on in my room. Grinning, he hurries inside, closing it behind him and pressing his back on it.

"Both of you are insane." Saying it to no one, in

particular, another shriek comes from me when Narsi pops his head up right next to my face. "Oh my God. I don't need jinn, I'll die from a heart attack."

"Oh, and I found the poor creep locked up in one of the rooms. He was sniffling, begging to be allowed to see his mistress. I figured you'd want to see his ugly face, too," Cass informs me primly, still sitting on the edge of the bed with her legs crossed at the knee.

"Beelzebub tricked me, Mistress." The Trowe hisses angrily, and I jerk my face away in case he decides that he is hungry. Sidekick or not, his bottomless pit of a stomach is no joke. "He used a ward so I can't open the door from the inside."

"Okay, let me ask again." Taking a calming breath, I blow it out slowly. "Where the hell is Eric, and what the fuck is going on?"

"Your mate is with your father." Cass smiles brightly. "All of them left to go kick Mammon's ass. At the warehouse" she adds that last part as an afterthought.

Jumping off the bed, I almost fall face first with the sheet tangling around my feet. "I need clothes." Kicking the damn fabric off my legs, I scramble to get out of bed. "And my dagger. I need my dagger….and boots."

I thought you'd never ask." Cass giggles, throwing my pants in my face.

I stop turning wildly when the zipper slaps me across the nose, my eyes watering from the sting. Narsi thinks we are playing a game or something because he is running circles in the room, as well.

"Ouch." Rubbing my nose, I glare at Cass. "You'll break my nose!"

"It'll heal fast, Miss I'm immortal." Smirking, she chucks the top at my head.

"If you throw the dagger like that, I'll stab you with it in the boob." Snatching the top, I almost drop the sheet from around me.

"I don't need Eric breathing down my neck." George is out of the room so fast I think I imagined him.

"He is so scared of Eric." Cass laughs, unable to hide her excitement about coming with me.

"And you are not?"

I drop the sheet now that George is gone forgetting that Narsi is still here. One quick glance tells me he couldn't care less if I was posing for him as I watch him chasing his imaginary tail. Yanking a drawer open, I grab the first pair of panties I can find, pulling them on before shoving my feet in my pants and jumping up and down to get them past my hips.

"Well, not as much." Cass scrunches up her nose. "I am taking you where he told me you are not allowed to go, after all."

"You are not taking me." Pushing my head through the top, I yank it over my boobs. "I'm going of my own free will." Buckling up the boots, I look up at her. "How long ago did they leave?"

"About thirty, forty minutes ago." She moves her head left and right with a faraway look. "I think." She hands me the holster and the dagger, not blinking an eye.

I watch her face as I take them, but there is no indication that she feels anything by touching my weapon. How interesting. I thought anyone would get all greedy or unable to resist snatching it for themselves. My friend just gave me something to think about after I join my father and my mate to kick their ass for leaving me behind. Strapping the dagger on my thigh, I tie my hair in a messy bun. Better to keep it tight than to have demon claws yanking on it.

"Okay, let's go."

Cass almost skips out of the room with Narsi right on her heels. We find George leaning on the wall opposite my door with his arms folded over his chest. He gives me a nod after looking me up and down, and my eyebrows hit my hairline.

"At least most of you is covered." He shrugs as he falls into step with me. "Eric will be pissed as is, so no need to add to it."

Shaking my head, I follow Cass. "Where is Raphael? Did he go with them?"

"No," I see George shaking his head from the corner of my eye. "He and the angels left a couple of hours earlier. I heard them mentioning Gabriel."

A knot forms in my stomach. I'm really going to scratch Eric's eyes out when I get my hands on him. All of them know they stand no chance if a jinn pops up out of nowhere. If anyone gets hurt, there will be hell to pay.

"Stubborn jerks." Grinding my teeth, I run faster, almost flying out the front door.

Skidding to a stop, I stare at Cass. She is behind the wheel of a small silver sports car I've never seen before in my life, grinning at us like an idiot.

"Where did that come from?"

"She got a little excited as soon as they left," George grumbles next to me. "She disappeared and came back with it twenty minutes later. I think she stole it from someone's house. I'm sure she would've woken you up sooner if it wasn't for that."

"Sometimes, I wonder if I know you guys at all." Pushing the front seat forward, I crawl to the back with Narsi climbing in my lap like a Pomeranian.

"So do I." Cass laughs, and as soon as George folds himself in half on the passenger seat, she guns the sports car with tires squealing.

Chapter Thirty

The city blurs around us, my heart racing as fast as the little silver car Cass is maneuvering like a pro through the town. We are all quiet, surprisingly, and even my sidekick is keeping still, his mouth shut, too. That in itself is scaring me more than anything. Can he feel something wrong, or does he know something I don't?

"We'll just go there and help them out, then after that, I'll deal with Eric and his stupid idea of leaving me out of things that concern me." Unable to handle the silence any longer, I huff in frustration. "He can be such an asshole sometimes."

"Only you would think that." George laughs uneasily from the front seat.

"And you don't?" This I can do. A banter between George and me is a familiar thing, putting me at ease.

"Let me be clearer." Twisting around, he looks over his shoulder at me. "Only you would think that Eric is an asshole sometimes. The rest of us"—Flicking a finger between himself and Cass, he grins at me—"think he is an asshole all the time."

The burst of laughter that comes from me makes Narsi jump, his bony little knees jabbing me in my stomach. Grunting, I struggle to move him off my lap with no success, so I give up after he keeps wiggling a few times. Blowing harshly to get his curly hair out of my face, I slump in the seat. I can never win with the Trowe, not when he does what he wants when he wants no matter what.

"I can see that." Pressing the blond mop of hair on top of Narsi's head with both hands, I look over at George. "He is not that bad, you know. He just gets grumpy when I'm doing something he doesn't like." Baring my teeth like a fiend, I make both of them laugh, Cass glancing at me in the rearview mirror. "Which is most of the time."

Our laughter cuts off when Cass slows down the car until she is crawling down the street. We are not far from the area where the warehouse is, but there is still a good ten-minute drive. Pushing Narsi aside, I lean between the two front seats, blinking fast as if that will change what I'm seeing in front of us.

"Where the fuck did they come from?" George sounds incredulous.

"I have no idea..." my voice trails off as I'm digging my nails in the leather of the seats.

Rows, and rows of armed humans are blocking the street. Their heads covered in black helmets glint in the glow of the streetlights. Armored trucks are lining the sides so far back that my eyes can't see the end of it. None of them are moving, the plastic shields clutched in front of them like that will save them if shit has hit the fan.

"George, get out of the car." The whooshing sound of the blood rushing through my veins pounds in my ears. I almost rip the seat out, slapping on it frantically. "Get out of the damn car now!"

All of us scramble out of the silver vehicle, me yanking Narsi behind my legs in time to stop him from bolting for the humans. They still have their backs turned to us, oblivious that we can slaughter them all if we were the enemy.

"Come on." Running towards the clustered stores, I pull George by his sleeve, almost tripping him. "We'll continue on foot. I bet the idiots made a big show at the warehouse, and that's why the humans are gathered."

"Mistress..." Narsi hisses, and I jerk him by the arm to shut him up.

"No eating humans, you hear me."

"He actually looks freaked out by the humans." Cass is right on my heels, chuckling uneasily.

"We can cut through the back, behind the bank." George points at the tall building of The Bank of America, not slowing down.

His boots are pounding the pavement slower than my heart is slamming against my ribs. All sorts of scenarios are going through my head while we run as fast as our legs will carry us through the streets of Atlanta. When the surroundings become familiar, I know that we are almost at sight.

Taking a sharp turn, my chest hits George's back hard, sending me careening into Cass with a loud oomph. Narsi hisses, crouching low and baring his teeth at nothing in particular. Well, nothing I can see until I right myself, detangling my limbs from my friends. My head numbs when I look at what got my sidekick so aggressive and turned George into a statue.

The street where the warehouse is situated is surrounded by hordes of demons. All of them are larger than average, resembling the ones we barely escaped when we left Hell. They are pushing and crawling over each other so they can reach what looks like a clearing in the middle, right in front of the doors of the warehouse. I don't need to see them to know that's where my father and Eric are. Knowing that Colt and Beelzebub are with them doesn't help at all. No one can fight off this many bloodthirsty demons.

Not even the Devil.

"We need to start picking them off from the ends." Cass is crouched low, murmuring under her breath. "The more we can get rid of before they notice us, the better."

Yanking George by the arm so he doesn't stand like a "we are here" sign for everyone to see, I pull both of us close to Cass. Frowning, I'm debating if I should call Narsi to come closer but decide against it when I see him on all fours, his body swaying gently from side to side like some human-shaped snake. I'll add that to the creepy stuff he does out of nowhere.

"They'll notice us the moment they can smell us." George clenches his fists.

"It doesn't matter." Feeling the anger building in my chest, I know it won't be long before the ground starts shaking. They'll know they have company even if we stay where we are. "Cass is right. Let's pick off what we can before I can't control myself anymore. When you feel the ground move, you better run." Looking from one to the other, I make sure they understand what I'm saying. "And watch where you step. The street will be splitting."

"It's already split." George points at the masterpiece I made the last time I was here and lost my shit.

"Yeah…" Hyping myself up, I roll my neck. "It'll happen like that again. Just don't fall into it."

"You did this?" Cass breathes from behind me.

"Sometimes I can't control it." I offer her the understatement of the year in response. I can never control it, but they don't need to know that before facing off with hundreds of demons.

"Cool." My head jerks back, giving me whiplash when I hear her awed whisper.

"You and I have a different definition of cool." She just grins at my comment.

Shaking my head, I look back at the bodies crawling over each other, all aimed at the front doors of the warehouse. Grunts, shouts, and hoots are heard, but that's just about it. All sounds mix together, making a constant hum in the air.

"I'll take the right." George doesn't wait for an answer, nodding once and disappearing behind the tipped-over car on the street.

"I'm left." Cass lifts slightly and runs across, still crouched as low as she can get.

Crawling forward, I stop next to Narsi, eyeing the demons. All those assholes are here trying to kill those I call mine. Turning to my sidekick, I see how focused he is on the horde. The Trowe is not even blinking, yet he hasn't moved a finger ever since we got here. Like he is waiting for something. Turning from him to the demons still oblivious to our presence, I frown.

"You ready, Narsi?" I watch him like a hawk and don't miss the tightening of his narrow shoulders.

"Yesss." He is practically salivating, not taking his eyeless sockets off the horde.

"Go eat their faces." As soon as the words are out of

my mouth, I startle when he moves so fast I can barely keep track of him.

I hear the scream of the first demon when my sidekick jumps on his back, clamping his teeth to the side of the demon's neck. Pulling out my dagger, I join him.

Chapter Thirty - One

Twisting away, my upper body swinging in half a circle, I avoid being kicked in the head. Not all the demons are aware of being attacked from the back because their focus is still on the warehouse. Those that see my other friends or me don't find it necessary to alert their buddies, which works for me just great.

Slashing with my blade, I cut a deep line into the demon's back. He roars and turns, throwing himself at me with his head bowed like a raging bull. Jumping, I kick out, catching him in the face and sending him back into the group that hasn't seen me yet.

They see me now, and I grin at them.

These three were smarter, so they slapped a few others

on the back or shoulders, pointing at me. My heartbeat speeds up, and the look in their eyes and the sneers on their faces. George was right, I should cover myself more. A few of them lick their lips, eyeing me up and down instead of attacking, spreading around to surround me.

Maybe I shouldn't cover up more.

Lifting my hand, I twirl the glowing dagger so they can see it. "Playtime motherfuckers."

One of them turns and runs away as soon as he sees the blade. I guess not all of them are stupid. Clearing out my mind, I fall into a familiar pattern. Twist, spin, punch, kick, stab. Duck and roll, slash out, cutting off whatever is within reach, and then repeat the process. I taste my own blood when one of them gets a good hit at my jaw, the skin splitting on my lower lip from his rock-hard knuckles. It sends me stumbling back into another demon, his disgusting hands splaying over my bare stomach groping me.

Bile rises in my throat.

Flipping the dagger so that the blade is level with my palm, I pull my elbow back, sinking the sharp steel inside his gut. Hot blood gushes out, coating my fingers before I yank it out, spinning on the balls of my feet and headbutting him away from me. Stars dance in front of my eyes when my forehead connects with his jaw, but at least he drops on the ground, curled up in hopes of keeping his intestines inside his belly.

Eric's roar of pain snaps my head in his direction, the

bodies of fighting demons preventing me from seeing him. Fear grips me like never before, numbing my whole body. The distraction costs me everything.

My head is jerked back, a demon deciding that I wore my messy bun so he can grab onto it. I hate it when they go for the hair in a fight. It makes me extra angry. Grinding my teeth, so I don't scream out in pain, I twist around to face him. Claws slash at my side, my blood soaking the waistband of my pants. Another claw-tipped hand slams into my stomach, cutting through my skin and sinking in. I have no time to kill the abomination before a bowl of energy hurls into him, chopping off half his face. The demon screams a chilling sound, and Narsi grins at me, crimson coating half of his face.

"Eat the motherfucker."

Huffing a crazed laugh, ignoring the blood gushing from me, I don't wait to see what the Trowe does. Another roar of pain and anger reaches my ears, and my power surges through my body, leaving me breathless. The ground under my feet trembles, the quakes strengthening instead of slowing down. The shuddering drops me on my knees, and all I can manage is to cling onto my dagger, afraid that a demon will take it. More roars and screams sound around me, the malice from a dozen evil eyes centering on my body. Anger bubbles up, stretching my skin thin, and I start praying that my friends will stay true to their word, leaving when they feel my control slipping. Because it's not slipping anymore.

It snapped.

I feel the first claws ripping at me only for a second. I blink and they are gone, followed by a terror-filled shriek. The ground keeps shaking, and I barely manage to lift my head, wanting to see who will deal the killing blow. I didn't think it'll end like this. That my own powers will cripple me enough that I'll be as docile as a lamb primed for slaughter.

Instead of angry demons, a shadow falls over me, hiding them from view. Wondering if Eric realized that I'm here and came to my rescue, I look around, but all I see are demons running. Sitting back on my haunches, I look further up, and my jaw hits my chest. It's not Eric or my father protecting me while I'm down.

It's Narsi.

The Trowe has grown in size, easily seven feet tall and just as wide. His once-tiny body is bursting with muscles, like a bull on steroids, bulging out of his very naked body, the tatters of his clothing hanging like threads on his shoulders and ankles. His claws are as long as my forearm, and they swing around, slashing everything within reach. Another blast of power bursts through my chest, doubling me over and sending my huge sidekick toppling through the demons. I can hear the concrete cracking and splitting like an eggshell breaking to let the hatchling out.

"Helena!" Eric's roar is distant, but it makes my heart skip a beat.

Lightning crackles above our heads, the electrical charge splitting the skies a second before a deafening boom lifts me off the ground.

The jinn have arrived. My heart skips a beat.

Small hands grab my arms, dragging me to the side, and I see Cass's fear-stricken face. Lips pressed in determination, she keeps pulling my stiff body away from Narsi, and I can't do anything to help her.

Another bolt of lightning flashes in the sky, followed by an even harder boom.

"Jinn…" I breathe the word, but the other power that almost burnt Eric fills my chest, and I jerk away from my friend, not wanting to hurt her. "No…" Moaning my denial, I weakly bat her hands away when she reaches for me again.

"Stop struggling, Hel." Screaming at me, Cass digs her nails in my upper arms. "I need to get you out of here. Eric is coming."

I can't even warn her before Michael swings his arm, catching her on the side of her head, and her body flies like a doll out of my sight. The jinn disguised as an Archangel smiles at me.

"We meet again, Helena." Gloating, his eyes shimmer silver before settling on blue, and he dangles one of the angels that brought Raphael to the safe house by the throat.

"Fuck you." With difficulty, I push myself on my knees, holding the dagger close to my thigh.

"Tck, tck, tck." He shakes his head. "No manners." He snaps the angel's neck, dropping him like he is a piece of trash.

"How about you come closer so I can show you manners." Spitting out the blood filling my mouth at his feet, I smile. "Come, give me a hug." My body shakes from my shuddering gasps.

All the shouts and roars are slowing down, and I'm not sure if most of the demons are dead or the blood loss is making it hard to hear. All my focus is on the jinn standing in front of me, looking at me with pity. Rage burns inside me at that look on his face, my fingers tightening on the hilt. I'm ready to explode. My skin is stretched out thin, and there is no turning back from it this time.

I know it.

The jinn knows it, too.

His eyes widen slightly, and my smile grows. I can feel blood trickling down my neck from my ears. Dark spots are narrowing my vision, but the jinn's face is as bright as daylight.

"Tonight you die, girl." The jinn sneers, hunching over and reaching for my throat.

I keep my eyes locked on his, unable to move away to save my life. The muscles on my right arm that's holding the dagger twitch, the anticipation making it hard to stay still. From the corner of my eye, I see Beelzebub reach us first, jumping at the jinn with a snarl on his face. The creature in front of me just flicks his wrist, blasting the large fallen away like a feather.

My heart does one hard thump against my chest.

I still wait.

The jinn is now within reach, his tall frame bending down closer, the disguise flickering and showing me his true form. The beauty of him is breathtaking, and Beelzebub's words come to mind. "Evil has many faces, Helena."

"Helena!" Eric's scream is too close, but the jinn is in my face already.

I smile, making him frown. "I die to...tonight." Gasping, I stay focused on his face. He leans closer. "But you do, too." My hand jerks up, sinking the dagger knuckles deep in his chest.

A thunder splits through the night, followed by a bright flash, blinding me, and I fall on my back, the jinn exploding in a flash of light. My back bows off the ground, almost breaking me in half and the loudest scream I've ever heard rips from my chest, shredding my throat. I feel Eric wrap his arms around me, hugging me to his chest as if his embrace is enough to keep me from bursting at the seams.

"Where the fuck is Raphael!" he roars, and my father's worried face floats in front of my face.

"They are coming," Satanael says, reaching for me and gripping my limp arm. I don't have the heart to tell him that maybe Raphael will not come at all.

His touch helps slightly, but not enough to stop what's coming. Colt looks like he's seen a ghost when he crouches next to Eric, their faces the same yet so different. Next, George carrying a bruised Cass comes around, giving me the strength to hold on for just a moment longer so I can see them.

I want to remember their faces.

"Narsi..." Gasping, my eyes flick around, looking for the pain in the ass that is the best sidekick a girl can ever ask for.

The Trowe, thankfully in his standard size, pops his head over Eric's shoulder, his eyeless sockets shrunken in worry. I smile at him.

"Protect Shadow, Narsi." His head jerks in a half nod as if he doesn't want to agree but feels he must.

"Helena, don't you dare!" Eric shakes me, hurting my neck. "Do you hear me!"

Another scream is ripped from me, and I feel those horrible fires lurching up, wanting to be freed. To my horror, I hear voices, and when I turn my head, I see the armed humans nearing hesitantly to where we are gathered. Fear grips my throat.

"Please..." My eyes find Eric's.

My mate looks ready to destroy the world. I watch him change into his other form, the horns twisting on his head and his features sharpening. I wish I had the strength to tell him how beautiful he is to me like this. Evil does have many faces, but he is not one of them. A hot fat tear rolls down my cheek.

"You must control it." He grinds his teeth, his deep voice vibrating his chest.

"I can't." Another tear escapes.

"Raphael will make it." My father doesn't sound confident. I can also see it on his stricken face.

"Please…" I'm reduced to begging, but I can't live with myself if I kill everyone I care about, including the humans. It'll be a fate worse than death. "You promised."

Eric closes his eyes, pain and sorrow etched on his face. I can hear Cass sobbing quietly somewhere to the side and Beelzebub cursing up a storm. The rest of them watch me with solemn faces.

"You promised…" A pained moan makes me cough, splattering blood over my face and Eric's chest.

Eric looks down at me, and my heart rips to pieces when I see tears falling over the sharp angles of his cheeks. "I love you." His voice breaks.

"I love you…too."

He presses his lips on mine at the same time his hand presses at the center of my chest. I taste my blood and our combined tears when many pained roars split the night. Eric pushes the shadows inside me with one hard pump of his hand.

My heart stops a moment after he lifts his head, and screams at the Heavens…

To be continued

FROM THE AUTHOR

Dear reader,

Well, that was intense, wasn't it? The series are coming to an end, and we do have one more book to go. I truly hope some of your questions were answered, and the previous books make more sense now. If you liked the story please consider leaving a review. It's like giving me a virtual hug and I greatly appreciate it.

Clink on the link : Review here

The final, book 6 will be available shortly. We have to finish 2019 with a bang. :) I'm grateful for you. Thank you for being on this journey with me. For cover reveals, freebies, and other news sign up for my newsletter.

Click here: Newsletter sign up form

Lots of love,
   Maya xxx

ALSO BY MAYA DANIELS

The Broken Halos series- PNR/Urban Fantasy:

The Devil is in the Details Book 1

Speak of the Devil Book 2

Encounter with the Devil Book 3

The Devil in Disguise Book 4

To look the Devil in the eye Book 5

Better the Devil you know - coming soon

Daywalker Academy series - PNR/UF

Investigated Book 1

Infiltrated Book 2

New Blood Rising series- Dark PNR

Risorgimento-Rebirth Book 1

Rovesciamento-Overthrown Book 2

Riconoscimento-Recognition Book 3 - coming soon

Stand alone-Dark Fantasy romance/ Mythology:

The Cursed Kingdom

Hidden Portals trilogy- PNR:

Venus Trap Book 1

The First Secret Book 2

The Obsidian Throne- coming soon

Semiramis series-Urban Fantasy/Supernatural:

Who am I - Prequel to the Semiramis series

Semiramis Awakened Book 1

Semiramis Reborn Book 2

Semiramis The Vessel Book 3

Remembrance Book 4 - coming soon

Printed in Great Britain
by Amazon

61237567R00142